INTO THE BLACK

AYLA RIN: AGENT OF TERRA PRIME BOOK 2

JON DEL ARROZ

1

AYLA RIN FLOATED IN A VACUUM, ONE OF HER LEAST FAVORITE activities in the universe. Though her environmental suit held her oxygen and kept her temperature regulated, it still made her uncomfortable as she lingered in the cold, black space.

Her helmet had lights that cast upon the asteroids in front of her, and her wrists also had lights she could point in different directions along with her arms. On her back was a multi-directional jetpack, which allowed her to control thrust through space. Additional thrusters on her feet allowed her to point and slow her movement if needed.

At the moment, she darted around several human-sized asteroids, looking for her target. Even though her lights were bright up close, they didn't provide much illumination for the distance. Dozens of asteroids lay beyond, but her enemy could be anywhere.

As if sensing her thoughts, a tactical bot with pincer arms and a laser-cannon head popped out from behind an oblong-shaped asteroid about thirty meters ahead at her three o'clock. She was lucky she hadn't thrust too far and passed it.

Even though her helmet provided a rear-view camera just above her right eye, it had several blind spots and required her to turn around to get a good look, which could be more difficult in space than it seemed.

The bot shot its laser cannon, orange light speeding her direction and giving Ayla little time to react. Though the suit had minor shielding, she couldn't take too many hits if she wanted to escape.

She activated her food thrusters, pointing them slightly to the left to give her a quick boost toward an asteroid about the size of a small office. The laser sped past her, connecting with another asteroid and blasting it into bits. The debris scattered in every direction and some of the small pebbles hit Ayla's suit but caused no damage. The advanced polymer used in its construction gave it a fabric-like softness but the toughness of metal. It would take more than that to poke a hole in her attire.

The current asteroid in front of her acted as a solid cover. From there, she pushed off and backward, leveling her laser pistol toward where the bot had been flying before and pulling her trigger.

Her shot connected with the bot, hitting it directly in its laser cannon head, frying its circuitry and neutering its capability to be a threat to her. Though it could still move and get her with its claws, these tactical bots tended to move slower than her as a genetically modified imperial agent. She was in the clear from this threat, at least.

More of those bots loomed out there in the black. She had to get rid of them all to secure the area and make it safe for the Imperium. The only way out would be through.

Her jetpack fired, thrusting her forward through several more asteroids. Everything blurred in the dark, but she could see the outpost beacon in the distance. She was almost through, but just making it there wouldn't be enough.

Ayla's mask blinked red several times, tracking enemies in the distance. Two more tactical bots had caught her signature and began following her. Speeding through the field had drawn them out. She was vulnerable out in open space, but so were they. She just had to fire faster than automated systems.

Lasers blasted past her, lucky to have missed her suit. She hadn't even had time to dodge them before they came, but her momentum kept her clear of any danger for the moment.

She used her thrusters to spin herself around but maintained her momentum toward the beacon. It was an advanced zero-gravity maneuver, but one Ayla had performed several times throughout her career.

The sudden shift of movement while maintaining direction would have made a lot of people sick to their stomachs, but she was the type who could read on a pad while accelerating to a full G without vomiting. It was as much her nature as it was a practiced skill.

She raised her pistol and shot the bot to the left, which sped toward her in a straightforward motion that allowed her to pick off another one with ease. However, the second bot flew in the same trajectory and blasted its laser cannon directly into her suit.

Her display screen shorted for almost a second before rebooting and turning back on.

"Defensive shield power at sixty percent," the suit said.

Ayla trained her weapon on the other boat, still flying backward. The bot kept on her, its sensors locked. It would be difficult for her to get out of its sights at this point.

It fired again before she could get her shot off—and hers went just wide this time. The bot's, however, connected again.

Once more, her display blinked out, leaving her in darkness for a moment before resetting.

"Defensive shield power at twenty percent," it said to her.

This wouldn't be good. Another would blow a hole right through her suit and expose her to the vacuum of space. It was the peril of being a biological life form against a robot. They could exist out here in this environment. She couldn't without special help.

Ayla pulled the trigger to her laser pistol in rapid succession. One of her shots had to hit.

The bot fired again as well and, this time, Ayla used her foot thrusters to get out of the way again while several of her shots strung across space. She watched in hopes that she'd dispatched it and, sure enough, one of the three shots she'd fired connected with the bot. It blasted into bits like one of the asteroids. She was lucky it didn't have defensive shields like she had.

After the fight ended, Ayla allowed herself to take a breather and float in space. It had to be the last of them. She had thrust through the asteroids to draw out the tactical bots, which would have been programmed to attack moving heat sources. They didn't tend to hang back and wait in the shadows. But her contact hadn't commed her yet. Where was Jorus?

All she could hear was the sound of her breathing inside the environmental suit. The ebb and flow of air sucking in and going out again. What if her contact didn't come? Was there something else she was missing from this mission?

After a few more brief wait moments, she thrust toward the checkpoint. This time, she took a more leisurely pace through the asteroid field, having aligned herself to take a straight shot through all the objects to get there.

As she approached, she spotted a shiny, metallic, oblong object. It had to have a computer system inside and some means of communication. When she came closer, she spotted a control panel.

Ayla slowed to match the speed at which the object floated in space. It was always a tricky situation, and her suit assisted her in ensuring she didn't ram into the object or float past it.

She reached forward to slide the cover off the control panel, but when she did, something rammed into her jetpack from behind, sending her spinning off course.

The worst part about spinning in space was that stopping became very difficult. Ayla's stomach churned as she grew dizzy, but she had to do something before she blacked out.

She jammed on the control to turn on one thruster to stabilize herself. It engaged, slowing the spin until she could get the controls situated to keep herself steady.

When her vision returned to normal, she spotted the first drone she had thought she'd destroyed. Its laser cannon head was gone, but its claws remained operational. Apparently, its thrusters remained intact as well. The bot rammed into her again, clamping its claws onto her.

Though her suit's material prevented easy tears, its claws could do a lot of damage if Ayla didn't find a way to stop it. She couldn't grab the bot and rip it off her, so she awkwardly pointed her laser pistol downward, firing a point-blank shot at the machine.

It was risky because a stray blast or ricochet could tear her suit as easily as the bot could, but she didn't have time to worry.

The bot powered down when the blast hit its center, but the claws had already attached themselves to her. It would be an uncomfortable ride from here, but it would be better than exposing herself to a vacuum.

Ayla thrust forward, returning toward the oblong checkpoint device. She reached back for the panel controls, opening the hatch this time and keying in the sequence to give the call a clear signal.

Bright lights were turned on in the zero-gravity scenario room, and an archway led to a door. The asteroid field hung in the domed room, looking less daunting than they had moments prior. The wreckage of the bots floated in the non-atmosphere.

"You made good time, Ayla," said the voice of Jorus, her handler, which came through her suit's comm.

"I'm glad I'm up to your standards," Ayla said wryly.

"Took a little damage to the suit, though. If you do so when you're out in the field alone, you're not going to be able to get repairs. There won't be backup."

"There never is, and yet I've survived this long. As much as I'd like to be perfect, I'm still human." Ayla thrust herself toward the archway. As she came closer, she spotted some rungs to hold onto when the door would open for her. She grabbed ahold of those and turned off the thrusters.

"A genetically modified human," Jorus corrected. "The Imperium's finest agent."

Ayla rolled her eyes. "Are you trying to butter me up so you can take me out to dinner in New Dallas again?"

Jorus laughed. "Always."

The arch opened into a hallway that had gravity, along with normal lighting. Ayla pulled herself onto the walkway and let nature do the rest to bring her feet to the ground naturally. Then, the doors closed behind her.

She removed her environmental suit helmet. Even with all the cooling mechanisms, her red hair was sweaty and knotted. If only modern technology could help her always look fresh like she was a holo drama star. Unfortunately, she still had to use a good old-fashioned hairbrush from time to time.

Jorus stood there, shaved head, and with his augmented glasses, which he wore at all times. He had on a well-tailored suit, ever fashionable. He patted Ayla on the shoulder. "I meant it, though, good work. I can only think of one other agent who could possibly clear the bots and get to the checkpoint as fast as you could."

Ayla narrowed her eyes at him. "Who?"

"Agent Shaen, but that's neither here nor there." He motioned for her to continue along the corridor with him and started to walk.

"I haven't heard of him," Ayla said, keeping pace at his side.

"He's on assignment undercover within the Scorpio Alliance. Hopefully, he'll make some headway by the time you're done with your next mission."

"Which is…?" Ayla prodded with the question.

"What you're about to find out. Are you ready to meet with Admiral Daker?"

Ayla let out a deep breath. The exercise she'd just been through had been grueling, but in her position, she rarely had time to recover. Daker especially, she'd like to look her best for, given the last time they'd met, she'd had to incapacitate him. He probably wouldn't be looking too fondly upon her. "I'd like a shower first, but I presume time is of the essence."

"His time is limited. He's an admiral of the Imperial Navy, after all." Jorus stopped in front of a conference room.

"Very well. Let's go," Ayla said.

2

INSIDE THE CONFERENCE ROOM STOOD A TALL MAN WITH WRINKLES ON his forehead and a receding hairline. He wore the ornate dress tunic of admiral of the Imperial Navy, with a golden sash across his chest displaying his decorations.

"Ayla Rin," Admiral Daker said with a wry smile. "It seems like only yesterday I was threatening to bring you in for a court martial, unleashing the entire might of His Majesty's Navy against you in the case you fled."

Ayla returned a smile that was much more genuine. "Not quite yesterday, but I seem to remember a sinking feeling I might be in some trouble after our incident on the starliner."

The admiral narrowed his eyes. "When you stole my key to a superweapon capable of destroying planets after cutting the gravity to the ship?"

"Exactly."

Jorus slid past Ayla into the room, moving over to Daker and patting the admiral on the arm. "This was all part of an agency-authorized plan to capture the traitor who set a false Emperor upon the throne, as I explained in my report. Perhaps it's time to let bygones be bygones."

Daker had a little twinkle in his eye, which let Ayla know he was mostly messing around with her. "Well, the basket of fresh vegetables that she dropped off with my wife helped lessen the sting. Perhaps one more?"

Ayla bowed her head slightly toward him. "Consider it done, Admiral."

Jorus looked relieved, and Daker clasped his hands together.

"All right, then," Daker said. "Let's get to what's important here." He helped himself to a seat and motioned for Jorus and Ayla to join him.

Ayla took a chair to the admiral's left while Jorus flanked him on his right.

"A new mission," Ayla said. She peered at a holographic star chart that popped up over the table. "I don't see where you're sending me."

"That's because I'm not sending you anywhere, within the galaxy, at least," Admiral Daker said. He zoomed out the diagram to show the entirety of the Milky Way. A line shot from a star cluster somewhere in the lowermost quadrant arm.

"This is a transmission we intercepted from the Scorpio Alliance after you successfully disarmed their plot to steal the superweapon. It went outside the galaxy. In conjunction with what we discovered on your prior assignment with the immortality serum, we learned that our rebellious colleagues are in contact with an alien race called the Darmarin. Until now, we didn't know where these creatures originated because we hadn't seen them within the sphere of influence of the Imperium which, as you know, encompasses the whole galaxy."

Jorus leaned back in his chair. "And our limits of the speed of our hyperspace drives have precluded us from going to other galaxies. Which, by deduction, must be where alien intelligence resides."

All of this was information she knew, but it still seemed strange. There was sentient alien life out there, and she'd been the one to discover it. Moreover, the aliens were hostile to humanity. She did not want to worry about it, but now she had to.

"You want me, a spy, to head into the black of space where we've never explored to gather information? Wouldn't this be a better job for the military directly?" Ayla asked, glancing between Daker and Jorus.

Daker's lips twitched upward into a half-smile. "You've got a good head on your shoulders. No wonder the agency keeps recommending you for difficult assignments. Yes, it would be, but with you being the reigning specialist on the Darmarin, we figured we could use someone who had hands-on experience to head the mission."

He motioned the hologram to move to the next slide, which displayed the profiles of several young men. "These represent elite members of our special forces who we've handpicked in order to accompany you on this mission. Lieutenant Lansing, Master Chief Olsen, Chief Petty Officer Parello, Petty Officers Kleinman, Miller, and Richards, And Doctor Dolame—all specialists who you'll be getting acquainted with later, so don't worry if you can't remember all of their names."

"I have an eidetic memory," Ayla said.

"I stand corrected," Daker said, shifting the image again to show an elongated ship, compact with a ring for the hyperdrive. "Along with three additional members to crew a deep space explorer class vessel," he continued, "you'll head toward what we believe is the end point of the transmission we intercepted. Our long-range scopes can't see anything in the complete black of space between galaxies, so we will be flying blind. However, our vessel is equipped with state-of-the-art stealth technology, so these aliens should be as blind as you are."

Jorus clasped his hands together. "Any questions, Agent Rin?'

"Now I understand why I've been training so hard in zero-G combat situations," she said, shooting a slightly irritated look to her handler. "This mission gives me a bad feeling."

"Imagine what the chiefs of staff are thinking when the Scorpio Alliance is known to be contacting a sentient alien race," Daker said.

"Oh, I know far too well how easy they are to push into a frenzy. At what point do we depart?"

"As soon as everyone is ready. You'll be working with the team on training for penetrating deep rock installations in the absence of light and extreme cold conditions, which we presume we'll find out there in space. Once we're satisfied with training results, you'll go immediately." Admiral Daker stood, smoothing down his sash and tunic. "Now, if you don't mind, I have to get to my next meeting. I'll leave you here to discuss."

Jorus smiled brightly. "Thank you for your time, Admiral," he said.

"Of course. And, Ms. Rin, my wife sends her regards." Daker nodded toward her and left the room before Ayla could get a word in edgewise.

She'd been lost in her thoughts anyway, staring at the hologram of the explorer-class vessel on the holodisplay. Traveling between galaxies? That was the work of extreme scientists or unmanned drones. It was far beyond her paygrade. She would have been much more comfortable infiltrating a well-guarded Scorpio Alliance installation. At least then, she could do her damage and get out. But who knew with these aliens?

"You look worried," Jorus said.

"No kidding," Ayla replied.

"Would a cocktail help to calm their nerves?" He cocked his head at her with a cute and innocent expression. The man was relentless in getting her to go out but, oddly, he never made a move once he had her on one of these pseudo-dates. He was an enigma, but then, one almost had to be to rise up the ranks in the agency.

"I might honestly need one with a mission like this," Ayla said. She pursed her lips, staring at the ship, losing herself in it for a moment. "I'm used to going into situations where I'm not going to have any backup. Why does this feel so different?"

"Because it is. There're extraterrestrials involved." Jorus dropped his usual bright smile for a more somber expression. "A few months ago, we didn't even know they existed. It's been millennia, yet humanity has never encountered any life capable of real thought. Isn't it strange in all of the universe?"

"You're not helping."

"Maybe not, but it's something I've always considered. Especially with the Darmarin out there. Why haven't we encountered them until now? I'm afraid there are going to be much bigger implications to this mission than you or I can even conceive. There must be some greater endgame than simply messing with the Imperium's internal politics to get them to risk revealing themselves." Jorus stood, his smile returning. "Which is exactly why I'm going to get a cocktail or two and forget about it for a while. There's nothing to be done at the moment."

Ayla couldn't help but laugh at his antics. "A deep philosophical thought, and it's all a ruse to get me to go for a drink with you?"

Jorus shrugged sheepishly. "Can't blame a man for trying."

Ayla stood. She'd had similar thoughts about the mission, the Darmarin, and what it meant in the grand scheme of human existence. It frightened her, and a mission like this meant the Imperium depended on her to bring back good intelligence on these creatures. This was a threat like she'd never faced before—like no one had ever faced before.

"Fine," Ayla said.

Jorus's eyes brightened. "What did you say?"

"I said fine, I'll come get that drink with you. It'd better be something tasty this time. You know I'm picky and don't drink much," Ayla said.

"Of course," Jorus replied, motioning toward the door. "I'll take you somewhere special where they import the finest liqueurs made from the flora on Barrya VII. You won't believe the incredible flavor profiles they have."

Ayla walked out with Jorus, not sure what she was getting herself into—both in the short term and in the long run.

3

AYLA TOOK A FLITTER TO THE IMPERIAL MARINES PARADE GROUNDS outside the capital the next day. The location was near the spaceport, easy enough for the fighting men of Terra Prime to board their respective outbound ships in service of the emperor.

Various companies of troops marched across the grounds, along with groundcars, transports, and supply vehicles busily moving between the various training areas and their outbound destinations.

Jorus tagged along with Ayla, keeping a keener eye on this mission than he had in most of her past adventures. Even the incidents like the artificial intelligence rebellion of Laundar IV with their insane OVERMIND seemed like far less of a threat to the Imperium than what awaited her.

It had been hundreds of years since the Terran Imperium had encountered a rebellion that spanned several systems. Most of their troubles came from local governments that became drunk with power.

Those were the missions Ayla and other agents of her kind quelled as quickly as possible in hopes that news never reached the nets or expanded across the galaxy.

But this, the Scorpio Alliance, had popped up nearly overnight.

There had been rumblings for some time, but they struck in such a swift, organized fashion that it took the emperor and his advisors by complete surprise. It hadn't helped that the emperor had been replaced by a duplicate clone in service to the new rebellion, a matter only uncovered by Ayla's work. She'd barely managed to escape that situation alive and with the Imperium still intact.

Even so, this alliance still thrived and grew over the past several months. The Imperial Marines had to be deployed across star systems for the first time in generations. The system governors and military intelligence leaders had become too complacent and relaxed. The decadence of the Imperium had caught up with everyone.

Ever since news of the Scorpio Alliance broke, it seemed matters worsened in the Imperium. Shipments of goods across star systems had problems, and delays in space travel occurred.

They were minor issues, but if those problems continued, they could collapse a civilization in swift order. It had happened several times throughout humanity's history, and no one had forgotten the fall of the original Terra, Earth, because of the collapse.

She was letting herself get too caught up in negative thoughts. The mission frightened her, making her prone to doom and gloom scenarios in her head. But she was here to meet some of the Imperium's best and brightest. She cast her eyes across the immediate area.

Jorus had his thick retro-glasses on. Even though his eyes could be seen through them, on the other side, he could have an augmented display and, in this case, he didn't hide the movements of his pupils. He was reading.

"We should be coming across Lieutenant Rod Lansing in short order. He comes from the Tytax System, middle of a family of eight—his parents were certainly busy—joining the Marines primarily for educational benefits, hoping he wouldn't be a financial burden on his family. Noble enough a reason," Jorus said, pausing in the middle of the parade grounds. "His record is spotless, having led both exploratory missions and battles against Robeni pirates out on the fringes."

Ayla mumbled acknowledgment of Jorus's intelligence file. Now, she had friends within the pirates after they'd helped her stop a conspiracy against Terra Prime. Not all pirates were as kind as the ones she'd encountered, certainly, but Ayla couldn't help but have a soft spot for the group she'd infiltrated.

"Growing sappy about your mission accomplices in your old age?" Jorus asked. He was good enough at his job that he could read her, even if he didn't have actual telepathic abilities.

Ayla elbowed him in the ribs. "If I'm old, you're positively ancient."

"Touché," Jorus said through a quick breath caused by her movement. He doubled over to a small degree, exaggerating the pain.

As he did, several Marines approached them.

The largest of the Marines was over a head taller than Ayla, with muscular shoulders, which made his uniform tight around the top. He had a shaved head like a new officer and an implant over his left eye.

A crucifix protruded from his uniform which, judging by the way the chain landed, he had intended to tuck inside. A traditional religious man.

Interesting.

"You must be from Terra Prime Intelligence," the man said with a flat voice that sounded like he judged them based on Jorus's antics.

"The best we've got," Jorus said, not missing a beat.

"God help the Imperium," the Marine said, impossible to tell if he meant the words to be a joke.

Ayla offered her hand to him, nonetheless. "Special Agent Ayla Rin, and you are?"

"Lieutenant Lansing," the Marine said. He had a patch signifying his rank on his collar.

Two other Marines flanked the lieutenant.

"These are Petty Officers Kleinman and Miller," he said.

The two men looked a little thinner than Lansing, with dark features that made them look like they could have been related.

"A pleasure," Ayla said.

"We're looking forward to this joint mission," Jorus said, brandishing his usual, winning smile.

Lansing raised a brow. "I wasn't aware we'd be joined by more than just Ms. Rin?"

Jorus chuckled. "Oh, I'll stay safely here groundside. I meant *we* in the global sense."

Lansing grunted. "Of course." He turned his attention to Ayla like he was done with Jorus. "Kleinman and Miller are our special forces infantry. Their job is to guard us while we gather intelligence. The brass also assigned us a computer expert, an explosives expert, a medic, and a civilian scientist. We didn't get the details other than we'd be departing shortly. This must be one important mission to assemble such a crew."

"It is," Ayla said. She didn't offer more.

If the Marines didn't know where they were going or why, it would be something to brief them about once they'd departed. Otherwise, there would be too many potential leaks. When it regarded a rebellion and potential alien life working with them, Ayla understood the need for secrecy.

"We'll be boarding a top-of-the-line stealth ship, too, so I've been told."

"The Imperium is counting on all of you," Jorus said. "And we don't want you to be undersupplied." If he noticed Lansing's dictates for him, he didn't show it. "Though, I do have to be getting back to a meeting with the emperor's cabinet. Ayla, I wish you the best of luck. Make sure to check in with me immediately when you get back."

"You can count on it," Ayla said. She fought the urge to smirk as she considered Jorus extricating himself and dropping to the Marines, saying he was someone of high importance by stating who he'd be leaving them for.

"A pleasure to meet the three of you," Jorus said. He bowed his head ever so slightly before turning.

The Marines didn't return his niceties. They were a serious bunch, to say the least. Ayla had the feeling it would be a very long trip dealing with them.

Another group walked toward them—three men and one woman. The woman didn't wear the Imperial grays but had on a modest blue dress. She must have been the civilian scientist they'd mentioned before.

"Hello," the woman said brightly. She had blonde hair and was a little shorter than Ayla. She didn't appear to have any body mods or technology on her. "I had the pleasure of sharing a flitter to the grounds with Chiefs Olsen and Parello here."

"The specialists I mentioned," Lansing said, motioning to the two.

Ayla extended her hand and shook the blonde woman's. "I'm Ayla Rin from intelligence."

"Dr. Megan Dolame," the woman said, shaking her hand. "Invistech Research Lab."

Invistech was a leading corporation that had its hands in several technological pursuits. The government had contracted them to work with the Darmarin cadaver Ayla had brought home from a mission.

"Looks like we're missing the medic and our naval companions for the journey?" Ayla asked.

"Our medic had to perform duties at the hospital, and there was no reason to invite the shipmen," Lansing said. "We'll be the core team of the operation, even though I don't know what it is. They'll be the transport."

Ayla noted a tinge of sourness in Lansing's tone. The Marines and the Navy seemed to have a bit of a rivalry. "Good enough for now." She tried to acknowledge everyone present. "I can't state much about our mission until I'm given the go head, but we'll engage in some off-world training in short order before departing for our final destination. I can tell you this will be dangerous, and I appreciate all of you for your work and sacrifice here."

"It's part of the job, ma'am," Lansing said.

The other Marines muttered their agreement.

"I think if I've been assigned, I have some small clue as to what this is about," Dr. Dolame said. "I look forward to the opportunity to learn more."

Lansing crossed his arms and sized up Ayla. "You're a little small for a dangerous mission, don't you think?"

Ayla gave her warmest smile in return. "I've been genetically modified. I may be on the compact side, but my speed will match or exceed any soldier on this parade ground."

The lieutenant huffed. "If only we'd get the budget for premium modifications. I'd show the emperor the greatest fighting force in the history of humanity."

"It's used sparingly for a reason. We all remember the lessons of the Superhuman Wars from the dark times," Ayla said.

Lansing quirked a brow, seeming to have a little more respect for her, judging from the surprise in his eyes. "You're studied in history."

"A number of subjects. The Agency uses R.E.M. enhanced learning programs as well."

"Of course they do. Is there anything about you that's natural?"

Ayla glanced at the other woman present, a devilish look in her eye, and then back. "My red hair, of course."

She could have been offended by Lansing's interrogation and hostile attitude, but the lieutenant was feeling her out, seeing how easily she'd crack. One didn't get very far in this business by playing the victim. She had to be on her game at all times, or more often than not, she'd risk her death and the deaths of those working with her.

It was a lot like being a Marine officer, she imagined, but she wouldn't say it because of how the military men had their pride to manage.

Petty Officer Kleinman snorted at Ayla's response. Lansing shot him a look, and he closed his lips tight, stifling a smile.

Dr. Dolame clutched her bag at her side. "I know I'll be able to count on all of you if there ends up being any fighting on this mission. I won't be much use unless I can science some of our enemies to death."

Ayla turned her attention to Dolame warmly. She seemed like a sweet woman. "Those have been deadly words historically as well."

"Well, then," Lansing said, "it was a good introduction. Once we get more information on our departure times, I'll be sending a communique to your personal datalinks. Do you have any questions for me or my team?"

"I'm good for now, and I appreciate your thoroughness, Lieutenant Lansing," Ayla said.

Lansing nodded, then motioned for his men to turn. They moved together as a unit, Lansing bringing up the rear. "Dr. Dolame, you're with us. We'll set you up with guest lodging here on the grounds."

Dolame waved To Ayla before turning and following the others.

Ayla had worked with Marines before, and Lansing fit their gruff and grumpy archetypes fairly well. She'd be able to handle him, but the real question would be, would they be able to handle aliens?

Only time would tell, but for now, Ayla had to water her plants. It was summer in the capital, and she would be devastated if any of them wilted while she was home to manage their growth.

4

AYLA SPENT THE EVENING IN HER RESIDENCE. AFTER TENDING TO HER rooftop garden, she settled in with a good novel, something she hadn't had the luxury to do in some time. She'd lost a couple of hours to her reading, a romance novel among two of the Imperial aristocracy. Reading about others' romantic adventures had a bittersweet taste given Ayla's lack of any kind of relationship.

She'd also not had time for such pursuits, which made reading about such matters make her yearn for some companionship, but she also didn't want to settle or resort to some kind of need not to be alone replacing a healthy relationship.

The pirate captain Mihael, who'd helped her on her last excursion to the galaxy's fringes, had wanted her, but she couldn't be with a pirate when she served the Imperium. The best she could do for him was to get him a pardon for his prior crimes and hope he cleaned up his act. It had been nice to be pursued, however.

The thought brought a small smile to her lips, losing herself in thought and also losing track of her place in reading on her datapad. She decided to set the novel down and start thinking about her mission.

The brass wanted her to leave as soon as possible, and the Marines seemed capable enough, but they were so set in their ways. Lansing might not be prepared for the reality of facing aliens so far from home. She idly wondered how it would impact him once he knew the true nature of their mission.

She would have liked some more help than by-the-book Marines. The thought of her Robeni pirates on a romantic level made her realize it had been nice to have their support. Part of her wanted to call on Mihael and see if he and his crew would be willing to join them on this venture into the black between galaxies.

It would panic the military officers with her. They didn't like pirates even more than they enjoyed posturing between their various branches. She couldn't bring them in unless she suggested it to the admiral. Perhaps he'd listen to her unorthodox methods given the success she'd had employing them in the past.

Ayla took the control to her comm unit into her hand, deliberating on whether to call the man this late. His wife probably wouldn't appreciate the intrusion into their home but, at the same time, with jobs as high profile as theirs, they were never off the clock.

She inputted his comm frequency.

It took several moments to connect, but Admiral Daker answered in audio.

"Ms. Rin, what do I owe the pleasure this evening?" Daker asked.

"I had our introductory meeting with our Marine contingent this afternoon," she said.

"Does the late call mean you had a bad impression?"

"Nothing I didn't expect given my prior interactions with military men," Ayla said. She couldn't help but smile to herself, though Daker couldn't see it.

"But something is still bothering you, yes?"

Ayla nodded. "I understand the need for heightened security, especially with an alien threat involved with helping an insurgency, but I believe Lansing and the others would do well to know what they're heading into before we launch. They need to mentally prepare for what they're going to face."

The old admiral wrinkled his forehead. "No, I'm afraid that won't be possible. As much as I agree with you in principle, the potential of your mission getting leaked could tip the Scorpio Alliance off to where you're headed. They could send destroyers to intercept you before you ever left the galaxy. It's too risky, and we can't lose our top Marines, let alone our galaxy's most notorious special agent."

"I appreciate your concern for my safety," Ayla said with a smirk. "But the reality of the situation still exists. How am I supposed to accurately prepare the team without them knowing what they're getting into?'

"In all likelihood, it'll be simple. You'll head to the planetoid or asteroid in the dark of space and extract all the information you can find, like any other recon mission. If there is enemy weaponry, you'll use explosives to destroy it. The fact that an unknown alien species controls these doesn't play into any of the necessary information for accomplishing these tasks."

It sounded simple, but how many people even knew of alien existence? There'd been a reason the public kept the knowledge of the Darmarin out of the media. Too much information imparted too quickly could cause mass hysteria. It would upend the Imperium.

To that end, Ayla wondered why the Scorpio Alliance hadn't already revealed the alien existence. But then, they wanted to keep their newfound alliance close to the vest. Politics was beyond her pay grade.

"I understand your point, sir," Ayla said. Even though she didn't have to address him like she was one of his officers, giving some modicum of respect never hurt. "But with an alien fight, they will need to know some of the tactics used in fighting other humans won't work."

"Which is why you can prepare with drones and bots," Admiral Daker said. He had her on this point, even though she didn't like it.

"You'll allow us time to perform some drills as a team, then?"

"I was counting on you to suggest it and would have been surprised if you didn't," Daker said. A yawn came through the comm system. "Now, if you don't mind, I'd like to get back to bed. I'm finding myself waking up quite early to deal with the news of the day regarding these insurgents. I still think the emperor should allow us to drop a neutron bomb and wipe these planets off the face of the star map."

"Civilians," Ayla said.

"Technicalities, always." He sounded like he was joking, but was he? He probably believed in an acceptable level of losses to some degree. How could anyone in his position not? But it still sounded frightening coming from someone in such authority.

"I'll coordinate the drills with the team, then. Will I be able to bring our ship's crew in on this as well? We'll all need to work together."

"All the resources of the mission are at your disposal."

Ayla felt a little better that he seemed to listen to her advice, at least to some degree. But she still had her big ask. Hopefully, he'd been softened up enough and trusted her enough. "There is one more thing," Ayla said.

"Hmm?"

"I was thinking a mission like this should have some backup. If something goes wrong with us, we'll be in between galaxies with no possible way out. If there could be a secondary ship on standby—"

"The military doesn't have the resources to expend more without diverting from our crucial front systems. I'm afraid it won't be possible," Daker said.

"I understand that. I'm going to suggest something unorthodox." Ayla took a deep breath, hoping this wouldn't be taken wrong. "On one of my previous missions, I made friends with a group of Robeni pirates. As odd as it sounds, they're loyal to the Imperium, and I'm sure they'd be willing to help us."

"Pirates? Knowing about a mission this crucial?" Daker laughed. "You must be out of your mind."

"I can have Jorus share my mission report with you from when I first discovered the Darmarin. These pirates are aware of the aliens' existence, and they've helped me before. Given the circumstances, I think they're the safest people from a classification perspective to act as backups."

"I'm not comfortable with authorizing this..." the admiral paused, "officially."

Her years as an agent made Ayla keen on discerning someone's meaning through tone. The admiral lingering on the word officially was all she needed to be able to pursue speaking with Mihael and his crew again unofficially. She'd have to keep this to herself. "Understood, Admiral," Ayla said cordially.

"Your unorthodox ways of managing missions have been a thorn in my side before, Ms. Rin," Daker said.

"I'm well aware."

"Please, make sure that doesn't happen again. I don't want to be in uncomfortable situations with the gravity taken out from under me— and I mean that literally and figuratively."

"Say hello to the missus for me," Ayla said.

"Will do. Goodnight." The admiral cut the comm line.

Ayla leaned back into her chair. She'd gotten her marching orders for the next few days, but the idea of this mission outside the galaxy still made her uncomfortable.

There were just too many ways for this to go wrong, with too few ways for her to extricate herself from the situation if there were a problem. In past missions, she'd always had some kind of escape valve.

She tapped commands into her comm system, sending a message out for the *Peregrine*. She had no idea where the pirates might be, so she kept it simple in case the line was intercepted. *Mihael, I need your help. Contact me. - Ayla.*

5

AYLA STOOD ON THE BRIDGE OF THE I.S.S. *LYONESSE*, WATCHING THE holo-viewer, which had a three-dimensional overlay of their destination, Asteroid G-6X88, a rock about a twelfth the size of Terra Prime out in the Calliata Belt. The asteroid had a medium-sized military supplies depot abandoned for the last couple hundred years. This would be the location of her team's training exercise before heading off to their real assignment.

In conjunction with the Imperial Marines, the agency had set up a course filled with several drones and bots acting as enemy targets. It wouldn't be as simple as the zero-G mission Ayla'd done back on Terra Prime.

This could be filled with all sorts of surprises. The goal would be to get her unit to act as a team, retrieve a data crystal of information from the base, and then blow up any weapons caches they found before they could get tagged by their training enemies.

Captain Cullen, a man with salt and pepper stubble and dark black hair, stood beside her on the bridge, interrupting her thoughts. "What do you think, Agent Rin?"

"I think I'd better assemble the Marines below decks and get us working on our objective."

Those very Marines wouldn't know this was a training mission. They would think this was an important offensive against the Scorpio Alliance and that they'd be in real life or death situations. In some ways, they would. The drones they'd face would be live, with real weapons firing against them.

Ayla didn't like the prospect. It was too dangerous, and she didn't want to risk injuring or losing any of her newfound team. But the brass made a good point when arguing for live training—if they couldn't handle the programmed bots, how would they be able to face off against actual aliens?

It was a good argument that led Ayla to this ship, which would be her home for the foreseeable future. She might as well get cozy with these people.

"Lieutenant Cetera," Cullen said, "bring us into orbit around G-6X88."

A lithe man who looked to be in his early 20s tapped at the controls of the helm. "On it, sir."

Ayla nodded to the captain and stepped to the side toward the lift so she could let the shipmen go about their business. Once in the lift, she hit the controls for the third deck, where the Marines gathered in a conference room.

The soldiers hovered around Lieutenant Lansing, who had a holographic display of the asteroid on the conference room table. Dr. Dolame stood in the corner with her arms crossed.

When Ayla entered, the men all looked up at her.

"Nice of you to join us, Agent Rin," Lansing said.

Did he have malice in his voice? Or Jealousy? She couldn't tell, but she had been busy on the bridge. She would have to earn this man's respect one way or another.

"Thank you," she said curtly. "We've arrived at our destination, as I'm sure you're aware. It's time to prepare the team to drop into vacuum and descend upon the asteroid. We'll be met with unknown threats and defense systems, and we'll need to extract a data crystal containing vital information to the Imperium from the main computer core inside. Once complete, we'll rig the asteroid with explosives to make sure any weapons caches are destroyed so the Scorpio Alliance can't make use of them. Any questions?"

The Marines shook their heads and muttered, "No, ma'am."

Lansing stood. "Excellent. File in. Head to the equipment stores to get your pressure suits."

The Marines fell into line one by one, trained, precise, and orderly. Lansing had commanded these men well. They marched out of the conference room, leaving Lansing, Ayla, and Dolame alone.

"I don't like this shared command situation," Lansing said, "but it's what's ordered, so I will tolerate it. When it comes to life or death situations in the field, however, I'll expect you to allow me to maneuver my men as I see fit."

Ayla bowed her head ever so slightly. "I wouldn't dream of another way. You command them well, Lieutenant."

The Marine nodded and followed the others out into the corridor.

Dolame still stood leaning against the back wall of the conference room. "I'm a little confused about why I'm on this mission. I don't think my expertise is needed."

"You'll need to go out at least to practice your zero-G maneuverability. These are trained professionals, and you'll have to keep up."

Dolame raised a brow. "This is just the beginning of our excursion, isn't it?"

Ayla ignored her, turning toward the conference room door. She wanted to talk to the other woman and explain the mission. As a scientist, Dolame knew full well that she was here to advise on alien matters with the limited information she had. But she had to stick to what she was ordered, for now.

Once they were on their way out of the galaxy to where no one could interfere with their real mission, she could open up to everyone.

"Follow me if you don't know where the equipment stores are," Ayla said.

Minutes later, the team had all put on their pressure suits and gathered their equipment for the mission. They moved from the equipment stores to an airlock.

The ship's engineer, Ensign Douglas, a stockier man than the others, stood on the other side of a forcefield that contained Ayla's team.

Douglas had a hand hovering over a control panel. "I'm going to be decompressing the atmosphere in five, four, three, two…"

The air evacuated with a *whoosh*. Maglocks engaged in the boots, making it so they wouldn't lose their footing. Within moments of the decompression, the bay doors opened into space, revealing white stars only dampened by black spots—the asteroids within their field of vision.

"Would you like me to lead the way, or would you rather?" Ayla asked Lansing in their suit-to-suit comms.

"I'll take point, thank you for asking." Lansing leaped out of the ship, engaging his jetpack to propel him farther. The Marines followed.

Ayla also turned on her jetpack, hanging back to make sure Dolame wouldn't be left behind. The scientist was tepid about going out into space and brought up the rear of the pack. She would slow them down, and it was Ayla's job to ensure it wouldn't cost them their lives.

With thrusters engaged, the team floated through space. With their suits, they were blissfully unaware of the cold outside. After some time, Lansing cut his speed.

"Parello, do you spot any perimeter defenses?" he asked.

The computer expert thrust himself to the right of Lansing. "There's a node at your six, and it looks like it's part of an external forcefield network," Parello said.

"Hold up, team. Let's get this disarmed before we fry ourselves."

Parello maneuvered himself downward, eventually shining a light upon a device about the size of his head. He tinkered with it for several moments, and then a pink light flickered where there had been an invisible defense shield before.

With the shield down, Lansing and his Marines resumed their flight toward the large asteroid. His men flanked him now, keeping their commander safe. Ayla kept back with Dolame. She hoped she wouldn't have to spend this entire mission—and she didn't mean just today—babysitting the scientist.

As expected, defense drones shot from the surface, zooming toward the group. The Marines spotted the first group of drones in short order, raising laser cannons and firing upon them with expert precision.

They blasted the drones out of space.

Ayla couldn't help but be impressed. She'd been so used to working alone or with some rag-tag group she'd assembled at the last minute that she'd never seen a squad of men make such efficient work of enemy targets. The Marines truly provided her with the best and brightest for this mission.

One of the Marines pointed to the asteroid. It was difficult to tell them apart in their environmental suits. "On the helm's ten-x zoom function, you can spot some kind of hatch going into the asteroid. The base must be inside there."

"Lead the way, Miller," Lansing said.

The rock surface grew in Ayla's field of vision as she approached with the others, and soon, it overcame space behind it. They touched down on the surface, engaging their mag locks to give them a semblance of false gravity and keep them from flying away by accident.

"Master Chief Olsen, I doubt we'll be able to pry this metal plate open. Why don't you show Ms. Rin and Dr. Dolame what you're made of," Lansing said.

Olsen crouched before the long piece of smooth metal his colleague noticed from orbit. He reached into his pack and produced a small device that looked like it didn't have the power to do much, let alone create a large blast hole. "Time for some fun. Everyone, step back," Olsen said.

The Marines moved backward, slow in their movements with their pressurized boots. Ayla didn't question them and tried to keep roughly the same distance as the others.

Olsen lifted off the asteroid, thrusting several meters skyward. A few moments later, the device blinked and exploded, leaving a giant hole in the metal plating where it had been before. The atmosphere rushed out of the hole.

"Looks like it was pressurized inside," Lansing said.

"My sensors are reading it's standard oxygen environment, safe to breathe if we can repressurize the area," Dolame said. The scientist's instruments were of some value for the mission, at least.

Miller slid feet-first into the hole Olsen had created. He lowered himself downward. "It's not too bad of a drop," he said before disappearing inside.

One by one, the Marines followed. Ayla motioned for Dolame to go first. She scanned the area to make sure no more drones or bots would be attacking them from the surface. Once it appeared to be clear, she jumped downward herself.

She hit the floor with enough force to bend her legs to stay upright. The interior of this place had artificial gravity, good to know. She adjusted her suit settings.

Kleinman engaged his thrusters to counteract the gravity and installed a mobile forcefield over the exit to keep the air in. The room repressurized as he landed again.

Lansing took his helmet off first. When he twisted it to open it to the atmosphere inside, it made a *whoosh* sound as the pressure equalized. "Pressure's good, but I'd keep helms on all the same. We can use the instruments, but who knows what the enemy might throw at your eyes?"

"Aye, sir," the Marines said in unison.

They appeared to be in a large storage area of crates and supplies haphazardly lying around the room. The only light came from their suits, illuminating small sections of the room. They needed to get lights on or power to the place before they could find the data crystal they came for.

"Any signs of computer components to get us some visibility?" Lansing asked.

"I don't see anything in the room," Miller said.

Ayla moved to what appeared to be a doorway. There was a small panel there with two analog buttons. One was depressed, and so she hit the others. The lights turned on.

"Looks like this is an old-fashioned bunker," Ayla said.

"It gives me the creeps," Dolame said.

As soon as she spoke, dozens of lasers blasted their direction. The Marines moved for cover with quick efficiency, but Dolame lingered behind. Ayla grabbed the doctor by the arm and pulled her behind one of the crates.

"Ow!" Dolame said.

"You can thank me later." Ayla narrowed her eyes toward the laser fire. Four security bots had repeaters firing, leaving no time between the different laser bolts for an opening. It always made tactics difficult to deal with machines.

Lansing made hand gestures to his Marines, a code Ayla wasn't privy to, and the two infantrymen flanked him. They reached into their pressure suit packs, and each produced grenades. Lansing followed by holding up three fingers, then two, then one, and when the last fell, his men hurled their grenades toward their targets.

The grenades fell a few feet before the line of bots but rolled to the metallic bases that acted as their feet. When they connected with the metal, they exploded, blowing each of the bots to their respective bits. It left two firing their repeaters, much more manageable for the group.

Ayla kicked one of the crates nearby to the side, giving the illusion that someone was moving in that direction. The bot reacted, adjusting its laser fire toward the crate. The shots disintegrated its target, but it gave Ayla an opening.

She raised her pistol, turning it to face the bot. With her augmented reflexes, she struck at the bot's central nervous processor, just above the central stem connecting its appendages. Her shot rang true, disabling the bot.

While she disposed of her target, Lansing picked off the other. His work wasn't as precise, his laser rifle hitting the bot several times before it collapsed from structural failure, but the larger blasts did the same job. It's not like they needed to keep the scrap.

Once the repeater fire stopped, Dolame poked her head up from where she had taken cover. Her eyes had gone wide, and she shook. "Wow, you're amazing," she said under her breath.

"We're the Imperium's finest," Ayla said, glancing over to Lansing, who gave her a small nod of respect. "In multiple regards. Looks like we're clear here. Let's proceed and see if we can't access the computer system."

Lansing closed a fist and moved his arm forward. His Marines understood the gesture and fell back into order, two-by-two, forging ahead toward the open door where the bots had originated.

They filed through the open area into a corridor that led to a smaller room at the end, handily labeled for them—Main Computer Area.

"Easy enough," Ayla said. "If we don't encounter any more resistance, we grab the data, set explosives, and leave."

Olsen managed to open the door through tinkering with the security pad beside it, and they found an empty room with a giant computer system. Several monitors had screens with cameras displaying other areas of the asteroid, but the base was largely abandoned.

Parello cracked his knuckles and stepped ahead. The others allowed the Marine computer expert to do his job, waiting.

Lansing looked over to Ayla and Dolame. He motioned his head toward the scientist. "The civilian is a liability, and there's no purpose to her being here."

Dolame opened her mouth to protest, but Ayla held up a hand to silence her.

"Listen," Ayla said, "this is just the beginning. She's an expert in something very important, and if you've seen how I work, you should know to trust me at this juncture."

Lansing huffed. "I don't trust civilians."

"Sounds like an iss-you, not an iss-me," Ayla retorted.

While they bickered, Parello completed his work, and the infantrymen set their charges. They were complete and standing at attention before Lansing.

The lieutenant shook his head, but then noted his men. "Excellent work. Let's head back the way we came in."

They filed out together, and Ayla stuck by Dolame. The scientist seemed upset, but she held it in well as a professional. Once these men discovered their real mission, it would be a whole different world, literally and figuratively.

For now, Ayla moved along with the men, hoping they'd be the ones ready for what they were about to encounter.

6

Captain Cullen sat in his chair in command of the *Lyonesse* while the shipmen took them to their stations. The trial run had ended. The Marines and Ayla passed the test and had some time to work together, but it still didn't feel like enough for the mission they were about to embark upon.

Ayla stood to the side, along a sweeping console across a second deck on the bridge. The captain had her in a special advisory position, though she wouldn't be much help for any of the ship's operations.

On the opposite side of the bridge stood Dr. Dolame, the lone civilian aboard the ship, looking as out of place as she had when she was out in her pressure suit on the asteroid. The Marine contingent's medic, Petty Officer Richards, handled her wounds without complaints.

However, the other Marines kept insisting she would be a liability toward their goals if she continued along with them.

Part of Ayla's job would be ensuring Dolame could make it out alive.

None of the Marines ventured aboard the bridge. The naval officers wouldn't have it, nor would the ground side fighting men be interested. They still hadn't been filled in on their true mission yet, something Ayla would have to do once they were underway.

"Helm, set us for hyperspace past the galactic rim," Captain Cullen said.

"Commencing hyperdrive in four, three, two, one," said Lieutenant Junior Grade Cetera, the helmsman.

A small power drain dimmed the lights for a flash of a moment as the ship reached incredible speeds out of normal space. Once in hyperspace, the ship could cross light years without worrying about any matter in between. It was a light and matter-bending expressway through the stars.

"Douglas reporting from engineering," a voice said through the comm.

"Go ahead, Ensign," Captain Cullen responded.

"All systems are functional, sensor masks activated. Though, I'm still confused as to why we'd need to upgrade sensor masks for hyperspace travel. It's not like anyone would be following us out this far," Douglas said.

"Classified business as always," Cullen said. "Thank you for your report." He tapped commands into his seat arm, which cut the comm frequency. Then, he stood. "We'll be underway in hyperspace for at least three days before hitting the galactic rim. Might as well make yourselves comfortable. I don't foresee anything interesting happening in the meantime."

"Famous last words," Ayla said with a grin. She'd been in situations countless times when events should have gone smoothly and someone threw a wrench in it. She'd be throwing one of her own soon enough.

Douglas might not have thought anyone would follow the ship, but he wasn't accounting for someone sending coordinates from the inside.

"I'll go brief the Marines on the nature of our mission. A few days of downtime for them to wrap their heads around it won't hurt."

Cullen nodded.

"I'll join you," Dolame said, stepping over to Ayla's side of the sweeping console. "It'll be fun to see the looks in their eyes when they realize why I've been brought in as an expert."

The two women entered the lift and rode down to the mess hall where the Marines had gathered. The hall had tables with a view of space outside, a kitchen counter where the ship's chef served them, and another bar for off-duty libations, which was empty as of current.

Though they wouldn't staff a bartender for this mission, Ayla imagined it would be seeing quite a bit of activity.

The chef was a portly woman, later in life, who wore a naval officer's uniform without any rank indication. She waved to Ayla and Dolame as they entered.

"Fix you up anything?" the chef asked.

"Not right now, thank you," Ayla said. She scanned the room for Lansing and saw him playing a card game with a couple of his subordinates. "If you'll excuse me."

She walked over to Lansing and watched the three men play their game without interfering. Dolame stood to her right, remaining quiet. Eventually, Lansing laid down his cards to display two pairs. Parello displayed a four-of-a-kind.

"Looks like I win again," Parello said with a smirk.

"Too bad we don't have any chips to keep track. We'll have to improvise," Lansing said. He looked up to note Ayla and Dolame.

"May I help you ladies?" he asked.

"Gather your men. It's time I brief you on the actual mission parameters for our escapade," Ayla said.

Lansing quirked a brow and held it for a moment before raising his arm and snapping his fingers twice.

His Marines came to attention, standing on the opposite side of the table and facing Ayla.

"I presumed there would be more to this than the brass let on. They were being too cagey with their non-answers," Lansing said. "It usually means there's something wrong or dangerous."

"True on both counts," Ayla said. "You've been told we have a top-secret mission that requires the best of the best for our budding war against the Scorpio Alliance. This much is true. But what you haven't been told yet is we'll be heading outside of the galaxy, into void space between here and Andromeda, where we have identified a small planetoid that has been sending transmissions with presumed enemy activity."

"Ahh, so our information retrieval and outpost destruction was a test run," Lansing said.

The Marines muttered to themselves, sounding confident regarding their recent experiences.

"I wouldn't think this is going to be too easy," Ayla said. "While we are familiar with the military capabilities of the Scorpio Alliance, this is a much more obtuse threat. This planetoid is believed to be populated by extraterrestrials."

Kleinman laughed. "I heard some reports of UFOs on the nets, but I figured it was just chatter."

Ayla met the infantryman's eyes. "It wasn't just chatter. The vessel is very real, and I've seen it with my own eyes."

The Marines looked at each other. Parello spoke up, "Is this some kind of joke?"

"I know a good one," Olsen interjected. "What do aliens eat? Unidentified *frying* objects." He laughed hard at his comment, but none of the others die.

"No joke," Dolame said, breaking the awkward silence that followed Olsen's corny pun. "I was the scientist brought in to dissect the creature and learn of its physiology. That's why I've been brought on this mission."

"Ahh," Lansing said without judgment. "This is making a lot more sense."

"You believe them?" Kleinman said.

"Why would they lie to us about something this important?" Lansing asked. "This is an interesting development. While I believe we're prepared to deal with any threat within the Imperium, it would have been beneficial to know what we were going into ahead of time."

"The admiralty thought the prospect of leaks regarding this information was too sensitive to risk it before we entered hyperspace," Ayla said.

"Prudent, though my men are trustworthy." Lansing sounded irritated.

"I understand why you'd be annoyed, but we were all following orders."

Lansing turned his attention to Dolame. "I'll want all of your data on the alien species so we might be able to better prepare a plan of attack against these creatures should the need arise."

Dolame nodded. "You'll have all of my notes uploaded to your personal datapads."

Parello shook his head. "This is crazy. We're going out of the galaxy to fight aliens."

"A suicide mission," Kleinman said.

Lansing huffed. "We don't know that it's anything of the sort. We'll retrieve the information on whatever's being broadcast from this facility, destroy it, and that will be that. I presume our mission is the same parameters as what we just worked on in our test run?"

"Yes," Ayla said. Lansing was very intuitive, and he'd been good in battle so far. The brass had picked a good team.

"And how long do we have until we reach our target location?" Lansing looked between his men.

"We have three days until we're out of the galaxy, and I believe another three days of hyperspace until we reach the planetoid," Ayla said.

"It doesn't leave us much time to study or prepare," Lansing said. He slid his cards across the table. "I think I'd like to get started on reading Dr. Dolame's notes, if you don't mind. This is unsettling information."

Parello scooped the cards off the table. "Of course, when I'm winning. Just my luck."

"I'll buy you a pint when we get back home," Lansing said.

"Deal."

Ayla noted the two men and exhaled. "All right. If you don't have more questions for me, I'll be heading toward my quarters. Even though this is a tough situation, rest up as best as you can. We'll need you fresh when we reach the planetoid.".

Olsen scoffed. "Like we'll be able to sleep knowing we're going to some alien stronghold."

The others muttered their agreements with Olsen, but Ayla wouldn't engage in any negative spriraling with conversation. It was unsettling news, but she couldn't do anything to change matters.

Going over their fears wouldn't accomplish anything. But she had one thing she could do to ensure their mission went as smoothly as possible.

She backed away from the group, and Dolame waved to the Marines, tiptoeing after her, catching up as Ayla reached the entrance of the mess hall.

"You weren't going to leave me there with them, were you?" Dolame asked under her breath.

The doors opened, and the women stepped through.

"I announced my exit, and you got out of there," Ayla said.

"They seem angry."

"Just annoyed. They're men. They'll get over it and be ready for action by the time we arrive." Ayla made her way down the corridor.

Dolame stopped at an intersection and said her goodbyes for the evening, and Ayla continued toward her quarters. She opened the computer and input command codes which would allow her to send a communication even while the ship was on lockdown. She typed in the frequency of her old friends in the Robeni pirates.

Mihael answered, his face appearing on the screen. "Ayla Rin, I thought I'd never see your face again. You seem like the love 'em and leave 'em secret agent type."

"Without the love part, perhaps," Ayla said with a smile.

"A man can dream. How can I help you?"

She explained the situation with the Darmarin, which didn't take as much explanation as it would have with most people because Mihael had been there. He'd seen the aliens and been involved in the action with them. He wouldn't be astonished by the reality of extraterrestrials.

"We're on our way to a planetoid outside of the Milky Way Galaxy, where we've intercepted the transmission. This is completely unauthorized, but I was hoping you might be willing to shadow us and act as backup?"

"Unauthorized?" Mihael raised a brow. "That means there's not going to be any profit in it for the crew. We're not a charity cause. Besides, getting involved in a classified mission for the Terran Imperium is dangerous. If we get found out…"

"You won't get found out." Ayla pressed her hand against her chest to demonstrate her sincerity. "Please. Everyone's lives could be at stake, including your pirates."

"This is a tall order, Ayla, even for you," Mihael said. "Let me talk it over with the others, and I'll see what I can do."

"I'm going to have to trust you'll be there," Ayla said. "I don't think I'll be able to make calls once we're outside the galactic edge."

"I'll do my best," Mihael grumbled.

Ayla blew a kiss to the screen. "Thank you."

"Mihael out." His image shut off, and the screen went dark.

Ayla fell back on her mattress, her mind reeling about the potential hazards of the mission. She was sure Lansing and the others were thinking the same things, but she hoped she could quiet her mind somehow.

Perhaps she should go back to the mess and get herself an herbal tea, chamomile…but then, she would run the risk of seeing the Marines again.

A small light blinked by the side of her computer, something which had been placed there while she was out and against her knowledge.

But Ayla didn't see it, too busy lost in thoughts. She turned to her side and shut her eyes without knowing someone was monitoring her.

7

Ayla sipped on sparkling water in the observation lounge. The streaking lines of hyperspace passed all around them, giving a breathtaking view out the side of the ship, which never ceased to amaze her. Dr. Dolame sat in one of the chairs with her, and the two women got to know each other while the Marines formulated a plan to deal with the Darmarin.

"How did you get into your line of work?" Dolame asked.

"It's a long story, doctor," Ayla said.

"Call me Megan."

She thought back to what seemed like ages past. Once she'd become an agent of Terra Prime, her life had been one crisis to the next, where time became a blur in her mind. "I worked in local law enforcement in the capital before. Jorus, who handles all the agents, found me and took a liking to me. He's got a fondness for women in general."

"One of those types?" Dolame looked concerned.

"No, no. I don't mind. It's flattering," Ayla said. "He is a diligent researcher, found I had a spotless record and offered me entrance into the program, along with a complete rapid-learning program and genetic modifications for reflexes and recovery."

"You weren't ever afraid that he'd mess with your mind somehow? I don't know that I trust those learning programs. They do too much in every sense of the word—programming, I mean."

Ayla sipped her drink, letting the fizz tickle her tongue before responding. "Maybe I've been programmed to some degree. Aren't we all? The way we were raised, what media we consume, it all influences us." She shrugged. "Sorry to get too philosophical."

"No, I enjoy it," Dolame said.

"I think overall, though, the Imperium is a good thing. It's humanity ascendant to the stars, all under one banner together. And Emperor Grigor is a solid leader."

"You're really patriotic." The other woman raised a brow at her.

"Somebody has to be during these times. I swore an oath to defend the Imperium, and I aim to keep it."

"Admirable." Dolame gazed into space, holding her glass in her hand without drinking. "I wish I had such conviction. I don't know. The Imperium's been good to me. They put me through school, landed me a job in xenobiology. I've studied creatures and organisms beyond most people's wildest imaginations, even with humanity expanding to thousands of worlds. There are thousands more where it's deemed too inhospitable for us to have a presence. Did you know that?"

Ayla shrugged. "I studied some in college science courses. I have a small botanical garden at my residence where I've amassed a collection of species from various worlds." A couple of her plants could leave an untraceable poison in an unsuspecting subject, but Ayla didn't want to scare off the doctor with too much information.

"It's pretty exciting, all things considered. I never thought, even with all I've seen, expected to be the first scientist to study a sentient alien species. The Darmarin's skin is a much harder substance than ours, more like a shell. Their legs end in points to stab into a surface, crab-like in some ways. I wonder what their world's like."

"We might get to find out," Ayla said.

Dolame stood, moving closer to the window to the streaks of

41

matter outside. "I thought we were going to some planetoid? Sounds like a quick outpost rather than their world."

"I've learned over the years never to presume a mission will be as simple on the surface as it seems to begin with," Ayla said.

She sounded so old saying it, but she'd been around long enough to be well-acquainted with the rules of engagement. One, nothing would ever go as planned. Two, one could expect everything to go wrong that could go wrong, even if it seemed impossible from the outset.

Improvisation and thinking on one's feet were the keys to success, which was why only a few people across the galaxy were qualified to become special agents. Most people, sadly, had no ability to think beyond their basic programming.

"Well, I hope to get back home sooner rather than later. I didn't sign up for a months-long expedition to another galaxy," Dolame said. "Do you have family to get home to?"

Ayla couldn't help but frown. One of the failings in her life had been on a personal level. With how busy Jorus kept her, she rarely had time to develop friendships, let alone romantic feelings. The closest she'd come in recent times had been with Mihael, the pirate captain who had been more than enamored with her.

Though she considered him a good friend and trusted him enough to have him tail them on this mission to provide backup, she still couldn't bring herself to let her guard down on a romantic level. Even though he was mostly a good man, Ayla could do better. The pirate captain had his flaws, but she didn't want to dwell on them.

"No," she said, her voice having more regret than she would have liked.

"Sorry to hear that. I'm engaged," Dolame said, volunteering a lot of information about her life. People tended to do that around Ayla, and she wasn't sure why. "He's a good man, another scientist I met with the corps. His specialty is in astrophysics, so we don't work directly together. Better that way."

"Mm," Ayla said noncommittally. She didn't have strong opinions on others' relationships unless something would obviously be amiss. "I'll try to get you back safe and sound."

Dolame turned to face her. "I appreciate you looking after me. The Marines don't like me. I can tell."

"Don't take it personally. It's because you're a civilian on a military operation. They don't take kindly to outsiders. They only tolerate me because I'm genetically modified to be able to keep up with trained fighting units," Ayla said.

"Oh, I know. But it's still appreciated to know someone has my back. This is psychologically taxing enough of an idea, going to some planetoid controlled by an alien who's helping tear apart the Imperium. The last thing I'd need is to feel completely isolated."

Ayla liked isolation personally, and while the woman was being sweet by all accounts, she wanted to extricate herself from the situation before they had too much of a bonding moment. She certainly wouldn't open up as much as the other woman wanted.

She stood. "I've finished my drink. I'll return my cup to the mess hall and call it an evening. Thank you for the conversation."

Dolame flashed her a small smile. "No problem. It was good getting to know you."

Ayla gave her a slight nod before turning and heading out of the observation lounge. She was better at these social situations when they were for a purpose or a mission. Something fake where she could keep her distance. This woman wanted real friendship with the real her. Why was it a problem?

It was something she couldn't spend too much time considering with their dangerous target only a few days away. She had to be ready for action, which meant she couldn't have too close of attachments with those aboard.

She dropped the glass off in the mess like she'd told Dolame she would do, and then made her way up to the bridge. With a hyperspace course set, the ship was running on an automated piloting mode, and no one else graced the bridge's presence for the time being.

The quiet brought her peacefulness, something she hoped would have come from the observation lounge, but she felt more at home with the ship's controls with the weapons nearby. It gave her a comfort, control. She liked control. Ayla grinned to herself. There could be worse nervous tics.

After a few moments, the bridge doors opened, revealing Captain Cullen. The man brandished a warm smile as he approached his captain's chair.

"Unable to sleep?" Cullen asked.

"I'm not due for another couple of hours yet," Ayla said. "But I am getting a little cabin fever inside the ship."

"She's a small ship, but a good one," Cullen said. "Being part of the Imperial Navy is a tough job. When you're a young officer, you get used to sleeping in little cubby holes with bunks and navigating through tight corridors. I can see how most people wouldn't enjoy such confinement."

"It's a lot like prison, I won't lie," Ayla said.

Cullen laughed. "In some ways, that's what the military is. But I also like to think it has its benefits. I get to be the first captain to fly out of the galaxy to encounter an alien species."

"But you don't get to tell anyone about it," Ayla said.

"Knowing what I did is far more important than having people perceive that I did."

Those were words of wisdom. Those who did often were at odds with the political types who took credit for the works of others. Hearing him gave Ayla respect for the captain.

"What do you think about all of this?" Ayla asked.

Cullen settled into his chair, staring at the viewer with the streaks of hyperspace showing from the ship's forward camera. "I don't know. I'm trying not to think about things too deeply. Knowing there are aliens out there from another galaxy who are trying to destabilize our Imperium is a heavy burden. These creatures could be the biggest danger to humanity we've ever encountered.

"On the other hand, if they could eradicate us themselves, they surely would do so rather than trying to pit humans against each other. It means they're low on resources."

"Or they just don't want to use theirs and are playing a long game," Ayla said.

"I was trying to be optimistic."

"I suppose a little positivity couldn't hurt. In my field, we don't get much of it," Ayla said. Almost every mission she had embarked upon in recent days had spelled doom and gloom for the Imperium. From OVERMIND, the rogue AI that was trying to take over humanity, to the crisis with an immortality serum to a recent plot to use ancient weapons to blow up Terra Prime, Ayla missed the days of simpler operations of uncovering corporate thieves and tax evaders.

She supposed, in some ways, it was better to do more meaningful work, but it was also a lot more taxing.

"I know I'll be happy to get back home when we're through. Though, with a war going on, the prospect of extended leave after a dangerous mission is probably out of the question," Cullen said.

"I bet your instincts are correct," Ayla said. She gave him a consoling glance. "I'm sorry, and I feel your pain for what it's worth."

"Misery loves company," Cullen said.

"I'll leave you to some peace and quiet," Ayla said. "I should reread the briefing reports and make sure I have everything down pat. Though, most of the information about the Darmarin comes from my lone encounter with them. So I'm not sure what good it will do."

"Never hurts to try to be too prepared."

That much was true. Ayla nodded to the captain and made her way off the bridge. Oddly, after talking to him, she felt a little better about the global situation. He didn't have answers, just worries, but they were in the same boat.

8

THE FOLLOWING DAY, AYLA WOKE UP BRIGHT AND EARLY—BY TERRA Prime Standard Time—and made her way into the ship's gym. It was a small room, lit brightly like the rest of the vessel, but with no view of space outside. It had a few weight machines, a treadmill, and elliptical cardio stations with mats for lying on the floor.

On one of those mats, Lieutenant Lansing lay prone before popping up into a pushup position. He repeated the gesture several times, grunting toward the end of his set. Sweat dripped down his face and covered the back of a loose gray shirt wrapped over black shorts. He'd been here a long time, apparently.

A couple of his Marines worked the elliptical machines where Ayla had intended to go, but she would settle for the treadmill.

Lansing looked up at her, stopping his pushups.

"Agent," he said with a relaxed cordiality.

"Lieutenant," Ayla said. "Getting a good morning workout in?"

The Marine officer shifted to a seated position, draping his arms over his knees. His ocular implant focused on her. "Figured I'd burn some calories and try to forget about this nightmare situation we've gotten ourselves into for a while."

"Nightmare? Surely, you've seen worse in combat," Ayla said, moving toward the treadmill. She stepped onto it and programmed the machine for a light jog.

While she wanted to ensure her body remained in shape, she didn't want to burn herself out in the days before going into unknown territory. She might need all her strength, and she didn't need to show macho bravado toward the men.

"I have," Lansing said, pushing himself to his feet. "But there's more to this. The alien threat. You may think I'm a jarhead, but I couldn't sleep last night thinking about the philosophical impacts of aliens existing."

"Oh?" Ayla asked. Then, she spotted a silver necklace with a crucifix falling over Lansing's shirt. She continued her jog while Lansing made his way over to her.

The Marine frowned. "Before I joined the Marines, I took a semester in seminary. I was going to become a priest."

"Priest to killer soldier? Seems an extreme change."

Lansing shrugged. "Not all men are as simple as they seem, and God calls us to act in different manners. What gets me about this is that men are created in the image of God. If you read into Genesis, you see that man is given rule over the domain of earth and all the animals. But if that's the case, what are aliens?"

Ayla huffed as her workout raised her heart rate. She hadn't been religious herself and certainly never thought of these questions on this level. Part of it scared her, thinking about the infinite, the unknown. As much as space beyond the galactic edge was infinite and unknown, it was quantifiable by the laws of physics. Spirituality was not her forte.

"You'll have to talk to the ship's chaplain or someone. I don't think I'm qualified," Ayla said.

Lansing raised a brow. "No? But you're an intelligent person. I could tell."

"I've met intelligent religious people and non-religious people." Ayla pushed her legs harder, and the speed of the program increased.

"For me, I couldn't sleep," Lansing said. "Hearing of the existence of these creatures racks my brain, and I can think of two possibilities for this. One, the creatures are some kind of demonic spirits."

"If they're trying to hurt the Imperium, I don't mind thinking of them as such," Ayla said.

"Two, though, is a tougher pill to swallow. If there are these creatures out there, and they have souls, and they're not mankind, it implies that reason, thought, and feeling are not things created in the image of God. It gives me doubts." Lansing frowned.

It was clear he was shaken by what he was saying to her. But why did he choose to confide in her? Was it some kind of test?

Ayla turned off the program to the machine to face Lansing. "Well, the writers at the time only knew what they knew. Perhaps the aliens are also created in the image of God, but just a different image? If He's infinite, then it would make sense He has different facets, right? And don't Christians believe in a trinity to begin with?"

Lansing nodded. "That was very astute of you, thank you. I'm surprised someone who's not religious has such a nuanced take. It gives me a lot to think about."

"I've had to study a lot of cultural matters throughout my work," Ayla said. "Sometimes we have to identify very specific traits going on within a group."

"And other times, you masquerade as someone you're not," Lansing said.

The words pierced Ayla. Lansing was smarter and more calculating than he let on. This entire conversation led to this moment, and he was trying to get information out of Ayla rather than the other way around.

The way he'd sounded so earnest at first had made her let her guard down momentarily, but she'd had enough experience as a special agent to know when someone was prying. But what was his end?

He hadn't trusted her since they met. That much was clear, but he couched his questions on God as a look into his soul. Was he trying to show her his truth while searching for hers?

"What are you implying?" Ayla decided to take a direct tack, hoping it would lead him to respect him more. They wouldn't have much longer waiting in hyperspace on the mission before they had to work, but Ayla hoped she could dispel any issues with him before they entered a hot situation with the Darmarin.

Lansing took a step back. His Marines still appeared to be working out, not paying any attention, but Ayla understood a setup when she saw it. They probably wouldn't attack her, but they viewed her as an enemy, someone not to be trusted.

"I don't like this mission," Lansing said. "The way the real nature of all of this was hidden from us. Aliens exist, and my team wasn't told about them before we left. As far as I'm concerned, the mission's botched before we even head out. Even with the briefs and the small amount of speculative research by your friend Dr. Dolame, we have no way to ascertain what the military capabilities of these aliens will be. It's possibly a suicide mission where I brought my best men."

Alya sucked in her bottom lip. She understood his pain but saw that he blamed her for the situation. He had to know it wasn't her fault, didn't he?

"I'm not the one in charge of this mission. It came directly from the military advisory committee of the emperor," Ayla said. "My handler was the one who told me I'd be coming on this. If I could have figured out a better way to prepare, I would have."

Lansing crossed his arms over his chest. "I understand how the bureaucracy works, but you're closer to these people than you let on. I've seen news holos where you're standing in the emperor's court. If you speak, they listen."

She wasn't sure how to respond. While it was true she had associations with some of the higher-ups in the Imperium, she did not have true power. She also didn't want to be continually on the defensive with this man, who had no real authority over her.

They were both chairing this mission in their respective manners, her as an independent agent and him to command his team. They had to work together, but he seemed to want to put her in a submissive position where she had to answer to him. Ayla wouldn't allow it.

"I think you have a misconnection as to how much power I have.

I'm a servant of the Imperium, just like you. I don't create the policy, I don't have a voice in it, I just execute orders," Ayla said. She hoped she spoke in a language he could understand.

The Marine stared at her for a long moment before huffing and shaking his head. "You might be getting us all killed for the troubles. Especially since we have to babysit a civilian doctor who isn't ready in the least."

Lansing turned and headed out the door. As soon as he did, the two Marines with him moved off their machines and followed him out the door. It gave the appearance the whole situation had been a set up. Were they trying to intimidate her?

If so, Ayla couldn't figure out the purpose. But these were Marines. Not everything they did made sense, and they liked to project a sense of power.

The whole situation left her uneasy, but she tried to put it out of her mind. She was here to get a good workout and settle her mind before the mission.

With the push of a button, the treadmill program started again, and the only sound left in the room was her running shoes hitting the mat.

9

Ayla's eyes glazed over after a couple more hours of studying Dr. Dolame's reports on the alien physiology. When it got down to genetic breakdowns and the hard, shell-like skin composition, she couldn't see how it would be of any tactical use in the field.

Ayla had been the one to uncover the Darmarins' main weakness—water. The creatures couldn't handle any moisture, so much so that they wore environmental suits around human colonies to keep any humidity away from them.

What a strange way for a creature to have existed. She couldn't imagine an existence with water being the deadliest poison to one's system, but this was why they were alien in nature.

After a short time of staring blankly at her datapad, letting her eyes glaze over, and the words and images blur before her, she finally set the device down. It wouldn't do her good to be able to go through these autopsy reports. It wasn't like they had much more on the creatures.

Their base of operations had been constructed with humans in mind, as the Darmarin were working with human colonists to try to create a subset of humanity under their control. Everything they'd found there would be useless in ascertaining the aliens' defensive capabilities.

They went blindly into the void.

It provided a stark reminder of how Lansing had been upset with her. It made Ayla doubt their mission. Perhaps they should have tried harder to devise a better strategy before diving out into the black between galaxies headfirst. No doubt this would be dangerous, but she knew that going in. So why did it seem worse now?

Because they were so close to it. In just a couple of days, she would be coming face to face with whatever the Darmarin would be throwing at her. So would the Marines. This was just pre-mission jitters.

She remembered to do her breathing exercises from training, one she fondly remembered as "the box." The intention was to have purposeful calm to try to lower anxiety. It consisted of four actions.

First, one took a breath in for four seconds. Then, Ayla held her breath for four more. Third, she had a four-second exhale. Finally, she held her lungs empty for four more seconds.

Scholars called this technique the box because as a person completes each breathing exercise, a person focuses on drawing a line each way to form a perfect square. The meditation worked by all physiological data, reducing cortisol levels and heart rate in a person.

Ayla spent the next several minutes working on the box breathing method before her door chime sounded. Who could be here at this hour? She suddenly became alert, sitting on the edge of her bed, looking at the door from the modest-sized quarters.

"Come in," Ayla said.

The door opened to reveal one of the Marines, Chief Petty Officer Parello. Judging from the look on his face, he didn't seem too happy to be there.

"Ms. Rin?" Parello asked, nervousness in his voice. The door closed behind him as he entered.

"You can call me Ayla. How may I help you, Officer?" Ayla tried to sound as sweet as possible. Whatever was coming, it wouldn't be comfortable, and he didn't look like he intended to flirt with her.

The man stood at attention as if this was some kind of formal military reporting. Ayla felt underdressed in her sportswear, sitting on her quarters' bed, but this was no formal situation.

She wouldn't be formally on duty until they launched from the ship, and even then, she still wouldn't be a technical part of the military unit.

"Yes, ma'am. Part of my duties involved in this mission is to oversee security, given the classified nature of everything we have going on here," he said. "When I reviewed the ship's logs today, I noticed an outgoing transmission coming from your quarters upon our departure."

Ayla hadn't taken precautions against being discovered. She assumed the ship's skeleton crew wouldn't have anyone looking into her communications. Why would they?

She was cleared at the highest levels and assigned by the admiralty. No one had any kind of authority over her on board the ship. But this could cause trouble with the Marines. They still had time before reaching the asteroid, and if the whole unit decided she was a problem, it could lead to her being sidelined, which would only hurt them.

"I had to check in back home," Ayla said with as cool a confidence as she could muster.

Parello frowned, clearly not buying her story. "I don't mean to be rude, ma'am, but if that's the case, why did the transmission get routed to Robeni pirates territory?"

"It was a security encryption." As much as she would have liked to tell him the truth, she couldn't exactly state she was contacting pirates to see if they'd come to help back them up on this mission.

The admiral already had a hard enough time with her when she suggested the measure, and these underlings would probably think even worse of her plan. In hindsight, she shouldn't have let her guard down and should have been more careful about erasing her below-board activities.

"I take precautions so anything our vessel does won't be spotted by usual channels."

The computer expert stared at her for a long moment. "I haven't heard of any encryption processes that work the way you describe, and as a computer expert, it's my wheelhouse," he said.

"Trick of the spy trade. If someone sees a transmission going off in an odd direction, it can lead them on a wild goose chase away from my true path. Protects any of my informants." Ayla offered a small smile. A soft feminine tack sometimes worked very well to lull men into a sense of security.

Parello nodded. "I'm sure there's a lot of tricks you have I don't understand. Please, if you need to make any other comms, run it by me first. I know the brass doesn't want our mission discovered by the Scorpio Alliance."

"I'm on the same page. Sorry to alarm you unnecessarily."

She could have tried to convince the man of her loyalty to the Imperium and mention all the work she'd done to date to thwart the Scorpio Alliance and their rebellious plans, but it would have only made her look more guilty.

He was suspicious, and talking as little as possible would make her come across as more confident. As much as she didn't like tricking the poor man, it was the best she could do for the time being.

He nodded, seeming pacified. "Well, thank you for your time. We've all got the jitters because of the aliens. I hope you understand."

"I do. I've come across them before, and it wasn't easy. I don't think I'll ever get used to it," Ayla said. At least she'd leave him with something truthful.

"Goodnight." Parello turned around, the doors opening for him to exit.

10

AYLA AWOKE TO A LASER PISTOL POINTED AT HER HEAD. SHE STIFLED A breath, but even though she'd been caught off guard while asleep, she had expected a similar confrontation.

"Do you have to be so dramatic?" Ayla asked, pulling the covers over her nightgown to be less revealing to the man who had entered her room.

"I treat traitors like the scum they are," Lieutenant Lansing said. He stood at the side of her bed, not leaning forward onto it, keeping his arms outstretched in a solid shooting position, which wouldn't allow her to reach over and throw him off balance.

"I'm no traitor, so you can stand down, soldier," Ayla said. "I'm also unarmed, so would you mind?"

Lansing stood still momentarily, but then stepped back to allow her some space.

Ayla crouched upward into a seated position, using pillows on her bed to prop herself upright and be able to look at him. "Computer, turn the lights to fifteen percent."

It had been dark, but Ayla's eyes were adjusted and altered to see silhouettes better in such an environment. Lansing likely had the same alterations if he was part of special operations for the Imperial

Marines. Now, she could see him more clearly, but she didn't want the room any brighter at this hour.

"You had to know Parello would come to me with what he found regarding your transmission," Lansing said. "You gave him some story about spy games, but when I had him look into the records, he found no signs of alterations. You were sloppy and thought we wouldn't be monitoring your communications."

It was true. She hadn't expected them to do much regarding her outbound transmissions. She hadn't taken the precautions she usually would have while deeply embedded in a mission.

Most of her experiences had been in places where she'd had to conceal her whereabouts with duplicitous people she had been tasked to bring down. This was quite different, working with a loyal military unit. The mission had made her let her guard down to some extent. Lansing and his people made her feel safe, but it wasn't something she could exactly say to him.

"Call it what you will," Ayla said. "You have a gun to my head, quite literally, but I'll remind you that I'm here with the full authority of the emperor, working as his special agent, equal to and given joint command with you. That's a lot of authority to give a traitor."

"The Scorpio Alliance was formed by one of the Imperial advisors biding his time and gaining a position of power and authority until he had all the pieces in place to form a full rebellion."

Ayla shrugged. "You have a good point. However, I don't suppose you'll likely believe me even if I told you the truth. You've been hostile since we first met, mainly because I don't have a military background. But I was a cop before becoming an agent. We might not have gone through the same things, but we have many more similarities than you realize."

Lansing grunted, not seeming impressed with her proclamation that they were similar. "You can begin by telling me the truth as to why you'd be sending a transmission to an area known to be infested by the Robeni pirates."

She tried to meet his eye and ocular implant, but Lansing didn't want to hold her eyes. It made it challenging to try to convince him of the truth. "I'm making sure we have the backup we need in case something goes wrong here. I have contacts everywhere in my trade."

"You're lying." He was predictable in his stubbornness. Why wouldn't the man just back down? They'd gone through an exercise together, and she'd spoken with him about the harsh realities they shared in this cracking of the Imperium. Why couldn't he just trust her?

"There's something here beyond just your general angst at non-military people," Ayla said, deciding to be direct about it. It's what he was looking for, right? He seemed to respect someone being straightforward. Politeness hadn't helped her so far.

"Yes, transmitting to enemy agents."

Ayla rolled her eyes. "They're not enemy agents. I would never betray the Imperium. I want us to win this war as much as you do. I know exactly what happens when empires crumble and how it goes for a way of life. The Scorpio Alliance is something made out of destruction. It's evil. The people in charge are evil. I brought down its founder personally. If you don't believe me on that, check my file. I'll even give you the proper clearance so you can see it."

Lansing stared at her for a long moment before holstering his laser pistol. "I've been betrayed before, and I'm not going to go into it. This is a military mission not a mental health center. But you can't act like you can be cavalier just because you're outside of the rank structure, either. I have men to look out for, and we're fighting for a cause. When I see a transmission to pirates, I'm right to call you out."

Ayla slowly nodded. He calmed down, and she didn't need to press him further. "Fair enough."

The words seemed to satisfy Lansing, but he didn't look happy. He stepped toward the door. "Since we're so far into space, I'm going to trust your story and hope you have a backup plan because this is a very dangerous mission with much less preparation than I would like to have given the gravity of the situation. But I'm watching you, and know that my team and I are diligent, and we don't miss the details."

"I've known that from the moment I met you, Lieutenant," Ayla said. "Have a good night?"

Lansing huffed and stepped out the door.

When it closed behind him, Ayla let out a deep breath she'd been holding. This had been very close to a disaster. He could have thrown her in the brig, and he'd have been within his rights, but wouldn't that have hurt the mission's probability of success? In all likelihood, he realized that would be the case and left her alone because he understood the greater picture.

Even though it was difficult having someone question her every move and be so grumpy with her, Ayla understood why the brass had assigned Lansing to lead an elite military unit like The Emerald Array. If anyone would be able to take down the aliens in a tough situation, it would be this squad.

11

"I'm reading a ship three clicks ahead," Parello said, manning the communications center of the bridge.

"Helm, bring us to a full stop. Maintain stealth mode so we don't accidentally trip any of their sensors. Parello put it on the viewer," Captain Cullen said, leaning forward in his seat.

The bridge became quiet with tension. Ayla stood at the back, waiting, while Cetera manned the conn, and Lansing took to the weapons station. It didn't help matters that Lansing was acting like Ayla was some kind of pariah, even now. Working together over the next few days would be difficult at best.

The viewer flickered from a side view of the ship traveling in hyperspace to regular stars. The camera changed again to the front of the ship, where the *Lyonese's* cameras spotted an object that looked like a saucer, metallic, cold, and blackened with debris that had accumulated on it for who knew how long.

The saucer floated in space, not showing any signs of propulsion, but its lights beamed out from different crevices of the ship, making a stark contrast.

"Any indication the aliens have spotted us?" Cullen asked, turning his head toward Parello.

"None, sir. We don't even know if anyone's aboard," Parello said, maintaining his focus on his console.

Ayla pulled up the schematics from the naval engineering corps of the first Darmarin vessel they'd encountered. It had high-powered laser weaponry like they'd never seen and a heavy plating on the hull, protecting against Earth weaponry and dampening any sensor capabilities.

The corps could only determine so much from their brief exposure to the first encounter with a saucer. The ship had been destroyed and wasn't salvageable to any great degree, much to the chagrin of the Imperium's intelligence agency.

"Is there any way to determine what's inside?" Cullen asked.

"Not without going in ourselves," Parello said. "My sensors are showing nothing from the inside."

Ayla could have told the communications officer that would have been the case, but she didn't want to interfere with the ship's operations, especially in a situation like this. She would wait her turn to be called upon and leave the ship matters to the naval specialists.

"I don't think anyone's aboard," Lansing said, tapping his console's controls.

"What do you base that on?"

"The ship's lack of any kind of movement. It's like it's floating in space. There's no propulsion, no adjustments, it doesn't appear to be on any sort of heading, and if it were in a waiting pattern, it would have been brought to a full stop much like we are."

"We don't know how aliens pilot their ship, to be fair," the conn officer said.

Parello furrowed his brow in thought. "Good points from both of you. This does seem within the scope of our mission to investigate this. If it is a dead ship in space, any information we bring back to the Imperium could be invaluable."

"It also could be a trap," Ayla said, finally deciding to give her input. She couldn't let the boys get too aggressive in this situation. They were outside the galaxy, and though she hoped Mihael and his pirate crew would provide some backup, she couldn't count on it now.

"It could be, but we have some of the finest special ops troops humanity has to offer with us," Cullen said. "Not to mention a top imperial agent. I'd like to investigate. Helm, bring us in toward the ship, and Lieutenant Lansing, let's see if we can't attach our little battleship to the hull of this craft."

"Aye, sir," Cetera said.

He tenderly brought the ship forward, lowering its trajectory so it would come up under the saucer when they arrived.

The alien vessel filled the viewer, the armored plating of the ship revealing its sheet metal cut lines and the bolts holding it in. There were some markings on the bottom of the saucer, which must have meant something in the Darmarin language.

As the *Lyonese* approached, it protracted three separate arms from the top of its hull, the end containing giant suction devices to secure itself with pressurized gasses toward the other ship's hull. The devices connected, and the *Lyonese* eased into place.

"We are successfully attached to the alien vessel," Lansing said.

"Very good," Cullen said, standing and turning. "Now to have your team work their magic."

Lansing moved from his station first, with Parello moving in behind him. Ayla watched momentarily, but then Lansing motioned to her to join them. The three moved to the lift while Lansing tapped his comm.

"Marines, we're heading out. Get to the airlock and bring your pressure suits. This is going to be an interesting adventure," he said.

The trio entered the lift, and the doors closed on the bridge, but Lansing didn't call to move decks. He turned to Ayla.

"Ms. Rin, I want to talk to you before we engage with potential extraterrestrial hostiles," he said.

Here we go again, Ayla thought. She tried to keep a professional face despite her annoyance with Lansing. "What are you thinking?"

"With this mission being such a variable, we shouldn't be bringing along a civilian—yourself excluded," Lansing said. "It's too dangerous."

He spoke about Dr. Dolame. He'd made his dislike of her as well-known as his animosity toward Ayla, but this was for a different reason. He believed the doctor to be incompetent. And Ayla couldn't say she'd blame him in first-contact combat situations.

"I agree with you to some extent, but she's also our foremost expert on these creatures. Her insight might be invaluable, from decoding their languages to navigating their ship," Ayla said.

Parello stood silent, and Lansing looked irritated. "I've read her reports. She barely knows more than you or I about the Daramarin. All she had to work with was some wreckage and a carcass."

Ayla shrugged. "Still, it's best to let the experts do their job."

"Which is why you're not part of a military unit," Lansing said with a biting tone.

What could she do? Dolame was supposed to be part of the team, and the brass placed her here because of her insight into the Darmarin. Even if the reports so far on the aliens had been sparse, it didn't invalidate her ability to perform her work.

"Perhaps we could compromise. Dr. Dolame, I'm sure, wouldn't like to be put into harm's way by going to an alien vessel where we might encounter hostiles. However, I think she should be given the opportunity to do the job she was sent to do. She's a competent scientist and should be treated with respect." Ayla crossed her arms over her chest.

"I'm listening," Lansing said.

"What if I kept in contact with her, gave her access to my pressure suit body cam, and allowed her to observe what I observe on the ship so she could take notes and advise us on how to proceed? She wouldn't drag anyone down on the mission, wouldn't present any danger, and we'd get all the benefit of her expertise."

"Seems reasonable to me," Parello said, breaking a moment of silence in the lift.

"Fine," Lansing said. He tapped the controls to head down to the airlock, and the lift began to move.

All discussion ended there. Ayla didn't expect the Lieutenant to be making friends with her any time soon, but she sure wished she could do something about his attitude.

Going into stressful situations with tension between team

members was never beneficial. But she wouldn't be able to convince him, and the best way to keep him at bay would be to stay silent.

When the lift stopped, they walked the corridor, entered the lockers, suited up, and returned to the airlock control. All the Marines stood present, and Ayla contacted Dolame to keep an open comm link, explaining the plan to keep her out of danger.

She didn't explain that Lansing was complaining about her. It wouldn't help matters. Dolame seemed relieved not to have to set foot on the alien ship, by contrast.

"You'll be my eyes and ears," the woman said, the words coming through in Ayla's suit helmet.

"Just tell me where to point the camera," Ayla said.

When the others assembled, the Marines decompressed the room and opened the airlock.

A hunk of metal stood in their way. The Marine specialists got to work using laser-cutting tools to pry a hole into the Darmarin ship. It would decompress an area, alerting anyone aboard to their presence if someone were around.

They might have to fight their way through the ship if things got hairy. This was exactly why Lansing took issue with the haphazard planning of this mission. He had a point, and Ayla appreciated his thoroughness, even if he could be a pain to deal with personally.

Kleinman turned toward Lansing while his fellow infantryman shut down the laser device. "We've created an opening, sir. We just need to push this hunk of hull inward, and we'll be able to get inside."

Lansing surveyed their work, floating outside the *Lyonesse's* gravity plating to ensure it was completed to his satisfaction. He then used his suit thrusters to turn and face the others.

"One the other side of this hunk of metal might lay threats beyond what you've ever encountered before. Stay vigilant, and don't get separated. We only have one shot at this, and if we fail, no one can bail us out. Understood?"

"Sir, yes, sir," the rest of the Marines said in unison.

They were a tight-knit group, for sure. Ayla watched as the men moved into place to knock the hunk of hull clear. They clamped their boots onto the area of the hull just below where the laser had cut, and together, they pushed inward.

The hull plating floated for a moment, and then crashed onto the flooring of the alien ship inside. The walls had a green and silver coloration, cold and alien. The lights on the ship shone in more of that green color.

"Are you getting this, Doctor?" Ayla said through her suit comm.

"I am. Interesting. Of course, their eyes might not be the same as ours. I wonder if these hues might be more comfortable for them," Dolame said.

"I'll leave the speculation up to you," Ayla said. She pushed off the deck to let herself fall into zero-G along with the men, floating toward the alien vessel. In a moment, they would be inside and see what lay in wait for them.

12

THEY ENTERED INTO WHAT LOOKED LIKE A ROOM WITH SHIP'S components. Pipes and wires protruded from the walls, along with flashing lights, that could have signified anything. Ayla had no basis for comparison among Darmarin vessels.

"Keep turning your head slowly and turn around three hundred and sixty degrees," Dr. Dolame said through Ayla's suit comm. "I'm going to create a 3D model of every room you go inside."

"This is going to get tiresome quickly," Ayla said, but she turned around as the doctor asked. As she did, the Marines watched her as if she were crazy. Fortunately, she didn't have to answer to them.

"Room's clear so far," Miller said, holding up his modified rifle. It had a flashlight on the end blasting light forward. All the Marines had them outfitted. This rifle, however, had a robust water supply to shoot from it, almost like a children's toy, along with its standard laser function. The Darmarin, as the oddest of all possible species, had a weakness to water. Their skin sizzled as if it caught fire whenever moisture hit it.

Lansing moved forward to what appeared to be a door. At least some things remained the same across species. Their door was more oval-shaped than the rectangular versions aboard the *Lyonesse*, but the basic function appeared to be the same.

He stood before the door, but it didn't open automatically. The lights in the room seemed to function, but if these doors were meant to open like the ones on the *Lyonesse*, they remained sealed for the time being.

His men surveyed the door. There didn't appear to be any recognizable panel, but a conduit ran from the left-hand side out into the wall.

"Should we open this?" Miller asked, pointing to the conduit.

"The only way out is through," Lansing said, nodding for them to proceed.

Kleinman and Miller proceeded to use the butts of their rifles to knock the conduit off the wall. When the metal came undone, it revealed several wires inside. The two Marines talked to one another but were unsure what to do in this situation.

"Are you getting this?" Ayla asked Dolame.

"I'm seeing everything and taking notes," the doctor responded. "It looks like their wiring is similar to ours, which makes sense because the principles of electricity should work the same. Positive. Negative. Ground, right?"

"I wouldn't presume materials on other worlds, especially other galaxies, work anywhere near the way ours do," Ayla said.

"Good point. Just commenting on how this seems familiar."

The Marines worked together to undo some wires and redo others. As much as Dolman's observations made some sense, there were more than three wires, and some had to operate the opening and closing system of the door.

Ayla enjoyed watching the men try to figure out the alien tech and stumble over themselves. Each wanted to be the hero who accomplished the task for Lansing's approval.

In the meantime, she decided to look around the room. There wasn't much around. It appeared to be some kind of storage area. Thin slits across the top of the room had to be air vents, which ran the entire distance of the room rather than being a duct that someone could crawl into like a human ship.

They must have been difficult to maintain. Likewise, the lighting came in soft ambient waves from similar recesses. The aliens liked it on the darker side.

What was odd was the absence of any computer terminals in the room. How did the Darmarin communicate or operate their systems? If someone was stuck in here, did they have no way to open the doors?

Thinking wouldn't give her any answers. They needed to explore this ship to find more.

The oval-shaped door rolled open as the Marines figured out which wires to splice. It revealed a wide corridor ahead.

"Got it," Kleinman said proudly. He turned and grinned at Lansing.

"Good work, soldier," Lansing said, motioning his Marines ahead.

The Emerald Array fell into line two by two, clutching rifles in case of any alien encounters. Much like this room, there proved to be an eerie absence of any Darmarin in the corridor. Where had all of this ship's crew gone?

As if to answer her to some degree, a forcefield shimmered into place where they had cut their hole in the wall. Ayla turned around to see a soft orange glow in place.

"Something just sealed us in," Ayla said.

Parello stepped beside her and glanced at the field. "It could be an automated system triggered when the door opens to the ship's interior. It would protect against the rest of the ship getting depressurized."

Something didn't sit right with Ayla. She pursed her lips. "If that were the case, wouldn't it have triggered when we opened the wall? This room depressurized, and there could have been people in here."

Parello shrugged. "I don't know how it works. Just speculating."

"Let's ensure we have an exit plan," Lansing said. "We'll head into the corridor, explore the ship, and see if we can find a place along the hull to the outside to use our laser cutters to punch a way out. Parello, let's get you to whatever functions as engineering on this ship so we can cut these forcefields entirely."

"Yes, sir," Parello said.

The Marines fanned out ahead of Lansing, moving into the corridor ahead. Ayla brought up the rear behind them, walking along with Lansing.

"They might not have a centralized control system like we do," Dolame said through the comm.

Ayla grimaced. "Let's hope their ship structure is intuitive enough."

The Marines opened another doorway, which led to what appeared to be another storage compartment, or perhaps these were crew quarters. The aliens didn't necessarily have to sleep in beds like humans, did they?

Olsen moved ahead to take point on the laser cutter device along with Kleinman, who held the back end of the cutter. They made quick work of this wall to open another hole to space outside.

The metal siding fell to the ground with a *clank*, dust rising into the air before it was swept away into the air filtration system.

Instead of the vacuum rushing beyond creating suction to disperse the air in the room, they faced the same orange forcefield that encapsulated the room they had entered. They couldn't get out.

"Parello," Lansing said, surveying the hole they'd created and the forcefield in front of it. "This field has to be generated from somewhere. Do any of your readings give us any clue on how we can shut this thing off?"

Parello shook his head. "I don't have any clue as to how this vessel operates. We'll have to figure it out the hard way."

"If the men all flip on their helmet cams, I can help try to ascertain the alien ship design and see if I can help," Dolame said through the comm.

Lansing motioned to the compartment's back door. "All right. Men, we're going to split into pairs to make this go faster. I think it's safe to say this ship is unoccupied, save for us. Look for anything that may explain where environmental or defenses might have some controls we can tamper with. Keep your helm cams on."

The men split up two by two, leaving Lansing with Ayla.

"Teaming up with me?" Ayla asked.

"Someone needs to watch over you. Let's get going." Lansing pressed forward along with Ayla.

Lansing seemed to be warming up to her. She hadn't tried particularly hard to impress him, but she found his distrust of her to be irritating. At times, it was hard to be cordial with him, but he had a strong sense of honor, and he always put the mission first before any of his personal preferences. She respected him for that.

As much as he wrote off the situation as watching over her, Ayla couldn't help but suspect he was beginning to respect her and wanted to team with her.

As the corridors split, different groups of Marines headed in different directions. Instead of a centralized lift, the ship had ramps up and down to different levels. As a saucer, it was much longer than the ship was tall, with only five different levels between the top and the bottom.

"I think I've got enough data to figure things out here," Dolame said.

"Go ahead," Ayla said, motioning for Lansing to hold his position while they listened.

"It's..."

"Sorry to interrupt. This is Captain Cullen," a male voice said. "We're reading a power surge coming from the alien vessel. It's building in intensity."

Lansing's eye went wide, and he had an odd look with his ocular implant unchanging. "They've rigged the ship to explode. This was meant as a trap. I knew it."

"Dolame? We need that info now."

"I'm trying to give it to you, but I was interrupted," Dolame said. "It looks pretty simple. From what I'm reading, the power stems from a central area on the second level above."

"That's close to us," Ayla said, motioning to the hall. She had a pretty good sense of direction. "We'll find it."

Ayla and Lansing jogged the corridor until coming to another oval-shaped door. It was closed, much like the one they had encountered before.

Lansing smashed the control pad with the butt of his rifle, exposing the wires. He made quick work of placing the right ones together to open them.

"You learn quickly," Ayla said.

"Have to think fast if you want to survive long as a Marine," Lansing said.

Before Ayla could respond, two drones flew through the door.

"The aliens have security!" Ayla shouted, ducking as one of the drones extended a razor sharp edge and swiped at her.

She raised her laser pistol to try to shoot it, but the drone fired its own laser, striking her weapon and forcing her to drop the pistol.

Without a weapon, Ayla was helpless against the drone, and the other flew toward her, flanking on the opposite side and extending a razor arm.

The second drone buzzed and flew toward her, aiming to lob her head off with its razor, but as it did, Lansing swung his laser rifle like a bat at the drone, hitting it with a resounding *crack* and forcing the drone off course to smash into the wall beside Ayla.

Lansing quickly steadied his rifle into his hands, taking aim for the first drone as it swooped toward Ayla's head once more.

Ayla hit the deck, aware that if Lansing couldn't stop the drone, she'd be in no position to defend herself. She had to trust him, though. He was one of the finest marines in the Imperium.

The sound of laser fire resounded above her, and Ayla winced. The drone fell to the ground in front of her, breaking into pieces, the deadly machine turned into a harmless hunk of metal.

Ayla pushed herself upward, her head about at the level of Lansing's knees as she looked up to him.

The marine offered her a hand.

She took it and let the strong man pull her to her feet.

"Thank you," Ayla said.

Through her helmet comm, Dolame's voice came through,

sounding distressed, "Are you still there? The energy build up is reaching critical levels."

"We're trying to get there. We had a slight detour," Ayla said.

"Try to get there quickly," Dolame said.

Lansing and Ayla entered the room together, the marine keeping his hands firmly on his weapon as he scanned the room for any other potential surprises.

This room had what appeared to be a lot of control panels, but the shapes and scribbles on them were utterly unrecognizable to her.

"Okay, we're inside," Ayla said. "This is where I'm going to need your help, expert."

"I've never seen their language before either," Dolame said. Her voice sounded tense through the comm.

"Whatever you're about to do, I'd recommend you hurry," Captain Cullen interjected through the comm.

Lansing stood astonished, looking at the control panels. "These could mean anything. We have no way to know what's what."

"Uh…" Dolame said. "Try the one just to your right. My AI interface is telling me it's an FTL drive control."

"They set their FTL drive to overload when we came aboard," Ayla said. She glanced at the panel Dolame had told her. "What am I supposed to do here? It's gibberish."

"You see the squiggly line next to the crescent?"

"This one?" Ayla placed her fingers by the symbols similar to what Dolame had described.

"Yes. Press those and slide upward, and it should cycle down the ship's energy core according to the AI. I can't verify whether any of this is right," Dolame said.

"Here goes nothing." Ayla followed Dolame's advice. The alien computer made some strange high-pitched noise back at her.

"Is that good?" Lansing asked.

"How am I supposed to know?" Instinctively, she looked up at what appeared to be some kind of energy core behind a transparent material shielding them from it. Nothing appeared to change in the chamber beyond.

"*Lyonesse*, how are the energy readings?" Ayla asked.

"Still climbing. You're about to—"Captain Cullen paused. Had the core energy caused some problems with their communications?

"Sorry," Cullen said. "Our readings are showing the energy levels dropping. You're safe. At least as can be on an alien vessel."

Ayla relaxed her shoulders. They could have died if not for Dolman's help. She wanted to rub that into Lansing's face, but this wouldn't be the time to try to convince the man he was wrong about the scientist. "Okay, then, let's get to work trying to remove the force-fields and get the heck off of this booby-trapped ship."

Lansing left her and Dolame to analyze the alien controls to gather his men. They'd be able to get all the information they could off this ship now, far more than the one that had exploded in their galaxy the last time they'd encountered the Darmarin.

Perhaps it would give Dolame enough to work with to gain some real insight into who these aliens were and why they worked with Terra Prime's enemies to destabilize the Imperium.

13

When they returned to the *Lyonesse*, Lansing wasted no time calling an all-hands meeting for the conference room. His taking charge created an uncomfortable air, as they already had a tenuous situation where Captain Cullen had his command of ship matters, and Ayla had a co-command of the ground mission.

There wasn't a clear chain as to who overrode who, which would have been much easier if Lansing had deferred to her. She certainly wouldn't defer to him at this point.

Still, there wasn't harm in a meeting, even though her muscles ached after exploring the alien ship. All of them could have used a rest after the stressful situation.

But after changing out of their pressure suits, the Marines dutifully followed their leader up the lift and into the main conference room, where Cullen, Dolame, and a couple of the ship's crew were waiting.

It also would have been nice to have a shower, Ayla thought. Some of the Marines had some poignant body odor from their recent outing. She'd get used to it in a few moments but, for now, the smell of men who had been sweating in their pressure suits for several hours filled the room.

"Do you want to debrief us on what you found already?" Captain Cullen asked, seated at the head of the table.

"You can call it that if you want," Lansing said, sitting at the opposite end of the table while his Marines took vacant chairs.

It left an empty seat beside Dolame, where Ayla dutifully joined the scientist.

"We collected quite a bit of data on their language, ship design, and computer iconography," Dolame said with a bright tone.

"I'm glad you had fun," Ayla retorted.

"Fun is not how I'd describe this situation, even in jest," Lansing said. His lips tightened into a flat pencil line, and he looked like he was about ready to boil over. "As you're all aware, we entered this alien vessel on the pretense that it had been abandoned in the middle of space. It seemed a good opportunity to learn more about the capabilities of our enemy before we venture to this planetoid where they are supposedly launching several of their operations against the Imperium."

"Yes, we all were watching the situation as it occurred," Captain Cullen said. "But we are still traveling through hyperspace for a couple of days until we reach the planetoid, so I'm not certain why we need to rush to meet."

"Because I want to stop us going to the planetoid at all," Lansing said. This created grumbles about the room of confusion from the Marines and the naval officers alike.

Ayla was a little taken aback at Lansing's audacity to try to end the mission. He seemed to be pretty by the book and without a direct command, he didn't appear the type to take the initiative for himself to change orders. They were slated to go out there, so why change now?

On the other hand, he had voiced his dislike of the mission several times up until this point. She remained quiet to hear him out, as well as to gauge the reaction of others.

"It's our mission to go there, and we've already come this far," Captain Cullen said. "It'd be a dereliction of duty to turn back." He spat the last phrase almost warningly, appealing to Lansing's sense of loyalty to the Imperium. It was probably a good way to try to handle him.

"When we embarked upon this mission, we didn't know a crucial piece of information," Lansing said, staring the captain down. "What we came upon here was more than just a derelict alien vessel. It was a trap designed to capture our people inside, and then explode. There's a greater implication to what we learned because of that, don't you agree?"

The room fell silent, none of the Marines wanting to contradict their commander, and Cullen didn't seem to be following where Lansing was going with this.

"I'm sure you'll enlighten us," Cullen said, leaning back into his chair.

Ayla tried not to smirk at the way the captain handled Lansing. The brash Marine wasn't used to someone who could verbally spar with him. He was used to being obeyed or, at the very least, having someone be intimidated by his general presence. Cullen seemed to be having none of it.

"It means the Darmarin *know* we are on our way. They're prepared for us. They set this up to try to cripple us, if not remove us from the field entirely." He slapped his hand against the table. "But it also follows they're prepared for us to arrive at the planetoid. If we show up there, we'll be destroyed. My greater duty is to make sure my men don't just go into a situation where they're shot out of the sky in a tin can like this because our brass didn't know the full details."

"What do you recommend?" Cullen asked.

"We turn back and inform the admirals they need to bring a full fleet to this planetoid if they want to deal with these aliens. One vessel is too risky," Lansing said.

Ayla couldn't help but let out a small laugh. She'd been arguing they needed backup since they first took off from the mission, and Lansing had nearly branded her a traitor because she decided to take matters into her own hands. But that was the only way they were going to get reinforcements. Lansing may not have had the full picture from the opposite side of the galaxy.

Her minor outburst drew his attention. Lansing raised a brow at her.

"Lieutenant," Ayla said softly, trying not to sound too condescending, "I've already voiced these concerns to the admiral before we left. As much as I'm sure they would have liked to have given us additional support, the Imperium's resources are completely tied up in this situation with the Scorpio Alliance. In fact, we have no idea how things have been going back home the last few days. Has anyone checked the subspace broadcasts?"

"Then, we wait until reinforcements are available," Lansing said. "If the aliens support the Scorpio Alliance, we can crush that rebellion first, then deal with this greater threat. What are we doing here? Opening a two-front war? Against who knows what? These creatures might even be demonic in nature. We don't know anything about them."

Dolame cleared her throat.

"We know significantly more about them now than we did a few hours ago," the scientist said. "The basic principles of how they use electricity or operate ship systems. They're more similar to ours than dissimilar. Geometric shapes seem important to them, especially circular patterns. From before, we also understand they have severe reactions to water exposure. Their ship's atmosphere, from what we read, confirms that they have some kind of filtration system to pull moisture from their air and keep it completely a dehumidified environment. Our AI has also figured out their language patterns."

"So, we completed a portion of our mission," Lansing said. "We can return home guilt-free."

Dolame shook her head. "There's a major difference between an inhabited planetoid and what we've discovered via one of their vessels so far. The more data, the better it will help our science teams come up with ways to neutralize the Darmarin should they pose a bigger threat to us than anticipated."

"At the risk of my people," Lansing said.

Cullen inclined his head. "I'd be risking my people, too, but, Lieutenant, at this juncture, it's not our place to make strategic policies.

That's what the admiralty is for. It's our job to execute orders they give to us. Even if it means something we deem dangerous."

Lansing's jaw tightened, and his natural eye filled with fire, but Captain Cullen's words stopped his protesting. The Marine had a point. They were moving toward very dangerous and uncharted waters, but they also had their loyalty to consider.

His ideals and duties toward the Imperium would win out for someone as honorable as Lansing. For all his faults, pushiness, and anger against her, he was a good man.

"You're right," Lansing said, which had to have been the hardest words for him to utter, given the tone in which he said them. "I don't like it, though."

"You don't have to," Cullen said. "But knowing what we know, we can be as cautious as possible. The *Lyonesse* is outfitted with top-of-the-line stealth technology. That's why this ship was chosen for the mission. Our approach won't be detected by any sensors known to man."

"*Known to man* is the key phrase," Parello chimed in with a wry tone.

Cullen shrugged. "It's the best we can do. If they know we're coming as it seems like they do, it might be a moot point, but our job is reconnaissance, and then destroying what we can find if we see something that's a credible threat to the Imperium. I want to get back home, and I'm sure you all do, too, whether that's to family, friends, or loved ones. They all are waiting for us. We all want to see them again. Are there any other concerns?"

He cast his eyes across the room. Several of the men shook their heads, but they remained silent.

"Good," Cullen said, standing from his seat at the end of the table. "It's been a long day, and I'd like to have a good meal, shower, and rest. I suggest all of you do the same. You did good work out there today. You're the first humans to go aboard an alien vessel and also the first humans to come back alive from the experience. Pat yourselves on your respective backs and know you've done a great service to the Imperium."

The captain's words had a calming effect, not just on how the others carried themselves but also on how Ayla felt more at ease. He had a good way about him, which she found admirable.

There hadn't been much time to interact with the ship crew, and perhaps Ayla would take the next couple of days of space travel to get to know him better.

The captain seemed to cast his eyes toward her with a small twinkle. Or was it just her imagination?

"Dismissed," Cullen finally said, and the men around the room got up to leave.

Ayla filed in with the others, finding herself walking along with Lansing. He was quiet, brooding over the recent situation.

Should she try to cheer him up? He didn't like her very much, but someone had to keep morale high on this ship, especially given the situation they were diving headfirst into.

"You know," Ayla said, trying to sound as casual as possible as they entered the corridor together, "it must be nice to know you have a God looking out for you in these situations."

She wasn't religious, but she'd heard Lansing refer to his faith, and if it comforted him, it couldn't be a bad thing.

He paused, looking toward her, eyes piercing as if trying to determine her sincerity. "You continue to surprise me, Ms. Rin," he said.

"Oh?"

Lansing nodded. "And the answer is yes, it is comforting. He'll watch over us, especially if I pray on matters. Thank you for the reminder. It makes all the difference, whether you believe it or not."

A shiver ran down her spine as he spoke with such conviction. She had given him the comment as something offhand, meant to comfort him, but should she be considering reflecting more on her creator? It was something she'd have to think about later.

"You're welcome, Lieutenant. I hope you have some good R&R over the next few days."

When they parted and made their way out to the bridge, alert sirens sounded, ending any possibility of rest.

14

"WHAT'S GOING ON?" CAPTAIN CULLEN ASKED AS HE RUSHED TO HIS command chair.

Lt. JG Cetera glanced back from the piloting station. "I tried to bring the ship back into hyperspace, but the engines shut down a moment later."

Cullen slammed the conn control on his chair. "Bridge to engineering."

"Engineering here," replied a voice on the open comm.

"What's going on down there? Helm is reporting we attempted to jump to hyperspace, but nothing happened."

The engineer paused and said, "According to my internal scans there's some dampening field outside of the ship keeping us from moving."

"Another trap," Lansing said, tapping the controls on his tactical station. "I'm reading an anti-hyperspace dampening web in the general vicinity. It's formed by dozens of nodes forming a field together and keeping us here. It's tricky. However, the readings are spotty. There's some kind of sensor mask keeping me from getting a lock on their exact location." He pulled his display up on the main viewer, showing the stars and hot spots, which appeared to be where the nodes were located.

"Can you shoot them out of the sky?" Ayla asked. It wasn't her place as a special agent to command the ship, but she figured Cullen wouldn't mind expediting any process to get them out of there.

Lansing shook his head. "I don't think so. The nodes aren't in a fixed location. They seem to be moving and the sensor masking will make it too difficult for our targeting computer. They appear to be controlled from a central node, however, in this general area." He zoomed in on a location to the aft of the ship. "It's camouflaged in the dark about perfectly. These Darmarin are sneaky creatures."

Ayla narrowed her eyes on the screen. She couldn't spot anything different than the rest of space behind it. But there was something there that kept the ship from moving.

"There's not much we can do from here," Captain Cullen said. "We'll have to go out into pressure suits to see if we can find someone to disrupt the signal."

"I can go," Ayla said. She might as well volunteer herself for something like this. She'd done enough training in weightlessness before their mission to be of use.

"We'll have Parello back her up," Lansing said. He contacted the marine a moment later via the comm system.

Cullen gave Ayla a slight nod of respect. "Good luck out there," he said.

"Thank you, captain," Ayla said. She turned to head to the lift.

IT TOOK several minutes to get herself suited up and out into space again. Parello floated in a pressure suit beside her, both with their suit lights blasting out into nothingness.

"I'm glad they assigned two of us," Parello said. "Out here where there's no stars, it's beyond creepy."

"We can agree on that," Ayla said.

"About your quarters before..." he started.

"Don't worry about it. I understand why you'd have reservations about me. I'm not offended."

"Thanks," Parello said, sighing with relief. "I do my duty, and the lieutenant wasn't sure where your loyalties were. It was suspicious, but after working with you, I've come to know you'd never do anything to hurt the Imperium."

They floated into the darkness, their thrusters keeping them on track to move forward. Even with their lights shining from their suit, there wasn't a sign of the node. Whatever tech they used to obscure the device might be valuable to the Imperium if they could bring it back. Not only did it obscure sensors, but it also hid from cameras and the naked eye.

"The Lieutenant isn't a bad person either," Parello spoke again through the comm after a long silence.

"I know," Ayla said. As much as they'd had some conflict, and he could come across as abrasive, Lieutenant Lansing shared a patriotism. However, he had the added burden of being a squad commander, where Ayla mostly operated autonomously. Naturally, it created a conflict in style. He was more by the book. In a military structure, it couldn't be any other way. Ayla, by contrast, often found herself rewarded for coming up with creative solutions to the Imperium's problems.

It would take some time for them to reconcile, but Ayla would continue to do her best to be positive and keep focused on the mission.

"You've been very kind since our first meeting," Ayla said. It wouldn't do any harm to be friendly with someone like Parello. He meant well. That much was clear.

"Well, once I confirmed you weren't a double agent betraying our position," Parello paused to chuckle, "I thought it'd be best to try to get us to work together as a unit."

"If your team would be kinder to Dr. Dolame, it would help," Ayla said, hoping she wasn't pressing too far. She knew the men hated having a civilian aboard who was functionally useless in combat situations. She slowed them down, but she also offered expertise in their field.

"I'll talk to the guys about it," Parello said.

Diplomacy. Easy enough. Maybe when she aged out of the special agent business, Ayla could get a nice post where she could put her natural charisma to use. If she survived that long, that is. Or if humanity did.

It hit her then, while floating in space, far away from any planet controlled by the Imperium, let alone Terra Prime, how much rode on the line. Their mission was crucial to gathering intelligence on the Darmarin, the aliens who pushed the Scorpio Alliance into rebelling and destabilizing all of humanity. If these aliens succeeded, it might not just be her who didn't survive. Trillions of others could have their lives at risk.

It suddenly felt claustrophobic in her pressure suit. Ayla took in a few slow breaths to try to calm herself.

"It's the best I can do," Parello said defensively as if her reaction was some kind of sigh to his statement.

"No, no. I appreciate what you're doing. I was thinking about the aliens."

"Oh." Parello then pointed. "Look ahead. I think I can see the node."

Something shimmered in the darkness, barely different than the rest of space behind it. But there was something distinctive there. Once Ayla focused her eyes on it, a diamond shape appeared. She adjusted her thrusters to move toward the object.

Once they came within a certain distance, the field obscuring their vision dropped, allowing them to see control panels, lights, and ports on the diamond object.

"It looks like some kind of holo projection field surrounding this. Smart use of the technology," Parello said.

"I'll leave the tech systems to your expertise," Ayla said.

Parello arrived at the object first. He produced a scanner device analyzing the node. "I can see where this is broadcasting the field, as well as the materials it's using to do so. It'll take a few moments to download the information. Hopefully, our engineering corps can reverse engineer this based on the data when we return."

Ayla waited for several moments while Parello learned everything he could from the node.

He turned to her when it was done. "Okay, I have everything I need."

"Did you bring any explosives to blast this thing into bits?" Ayla asked.

"Ahh. No one told me to. That's usually Olsen's job," Parello said.

Ayla considered what should be done in this situation. "I know. I'll plant my comm device here to give the ship something to track so Lansing can have something to lock onto from the ship. I won't be able to communicate until we get back, though. You'll have to call the bridge and tell them the situation." She removed the comm unit from her suit and placed it on the object. The comm unit magnetically adhered to the node much like it did her suit, saving her from finding a way to keep it on the node.

Once done, she gave Parello a thumbs up. He began thrusting away, and Ayla followed him. The *Lyonesse* hung in space in front of them and grew in her vision as they came closer. A bright light emanated and reflected on the hull, causing Ayla to look back.

The node was now a bunch of space debris. There was no sound in space to alert her to the laser fire from the ship, only the remnants of the alien device. They'd done their duty, and hopefully, this would be the last thing she'd need to do for a while longer. As much as she enjoyed being useful to the mission, she began feeling fatigued.

Returning her focus to the ship, Ayla pushed her thrusters to their maximum speed as she and Parello headed toward the airlock.

15

AYLA WOKE UP REFRESHED THE NEXT DAY. SHE'D TAKEN A HOT SHOWER with the ship's reclaimed water system and slept nearly ten hours. The stress of dealing with the alien ship had been exhausting. But after a yawn and a stretch, she got herself ready to go again, heading to the ship's mess to get a cup of coffee.

Cullen hadn't skimped on the requisitions for quality coffee for the journey. She found whatever brew they had to be better than what she usually kept at home. To be fair, she didn't buy the highest quality beans because they'd go stale with her out on missions and coming back.

It didn't hamper her vegetable garden because she sent people to look after them when she was gone. Priorities, she supposed.

With the little stimulant pick-me-up the coffee offered, Ayla found herself bouncing on her feet to want to work. All she could do was train her body by working out, which she didn't feel like doing after exerting herself on the prior day, or she could learn more about the Darmarin.

The latter sounded like the intelligent choice, so she headed to where Dolame had set up her makeshift science lab on the *Lyonesse*.

The room was filled with holograms, some of the Darmarin

vessels they'd encountered from exterior shots, a look at the carcass of the creature Ayla had fought, and then running video from her helmet cam's view on the alien vessel yesterday.

Dr. Dolame was seated on a swiveling chair in front of the video projection, with a datapad in her hand, taking notes as she came across different facets of the Darmarin's ship systems.

"Learn anything interesting?" Ayla asked.

The scientist turned around, startled. "I didn't hear you there."

"Even with the automatic doors?"

Dolame shook her head. "I've been immersed in the video for too long. I should probably take a break." She tapped her datapad, which paused the playback. Then, she wrinkled her brow in consideration. "As far as what I've learned..."

Ayla glanced at her pad with interest.

"The Darmarin have a pretty sparse setup with their systems. Not many redundancies like we have. I know humans have an immense fear of failure because we'd be exposed to the vacuum of space, which is never a pleasant thought. But perhaps the Darmarin don't have that fear? Maybe they can operate outside in a vacuum because of the way the hardness of their bodies are constructed, much like a shell."

"That's an interesting thought," Ayla said. The one thing she knew about them was their immense weakness to water, which allowed her to win a battle that otherwise would have left her dead. "They wear encounter suits in our atmosphere. At least the one I met did."

"True," Dolame said. "I haven't determined if there's a purpose because of their need for a lack of moisture in the air or if they used such to conceal their looks from us. The alien would have stood out because of an encounter suit, but he still could have pretended to be human in some regards to hide from the populace there."

"Or perhaps it's both?" Ayla asked.

"A dual function, which I see a lot of within their ship as well. They don't have a separate battery pack for life support systems like we do, but they have it tied directly into their engine core, which is dangerous. If something goes wrong, what do they do?"

Ayla shrugged without much thought to offer on it. "It looks like you're making good work at the very least."

"I'm trying to figure out their motives for wanting to destabilize the Imperium. Obviously, they perceive us as a threat to something they want. If they are so stingy with their resources, maybe they come from an area without abundant metals or minerals. Maybe they want to take ours?"

"I'm certain the Imperium would work with them as a trading partner," Ayla said. "There's no reason to spur a rebellion and create upheaval."

Dolame snapped her fingers. "If they had resources to trade, they wouldn't be in this situation. What if they're creating the rebellion in hopes we wipe ourselves out so they don't have to extend their resources on some kind of invasion? This way, they can take the resources from our galaxy without resistance."

The theory was pretty sound, even if there wasn't a lot of information to formulate it, at least in Ayla's opinion. Perhaps Dolame had a better mind for insights into cultures. She probably did since science was her vocation.

But could they do anything about it even if they understood the aliens' motivation for attacking the Imperium? It's not like the Darmarin were reaching out to talk to them.

Or perhaps that's what they should try here on this mission, actually talking with the Darmarin. So far, there had only been subterfuge from the alien beings, but it could be something they were doing out of fear.

If Ayla could get in front of them and convince them to stop helping the Scorpio Alliance, that it wasn't in their best interest for a destabilized Imperium, perhaps she could be a bigger benefit than she had ever hoped to be to preserve her civilization.

"I see your wheels turning," Dolame said.

"You've got me thinking," Ayla said. "But it's just a theory, right?"

"I've got some handle on their culture from the data our AI accumulated on their language in conjunction with what I'm observing. Well, culture is a loose term. The Darmarin don't seem to have any capacity for art or creativity from what I'm understanding of their language. It's very dry, no pun intended, with their aversion to water."

"If they're burrowing into planetoids in the black between galaxies, I can only imagine," Ayla said. "It doesn't sound like the best of existences."

"Perhaps that's what makes us seem like a threat to them. Our vibrancy, our capacity for culture. They could view it as an abomination."

"Another theory?" Ayla raised a brow.

"As good as any until we get more on them. I still have a whole lot of data we siphoned from their ship to analyze."

"I'll let you get to it, then," Ayla said. "Thank you for giving me some insight into these creatures."

Dolame gave her a friendly smile before returning her attention to her projection. The video started again, and the scientist resumed her copious note-taking of what she saw.

Ayla saw herself out of the room.

In the corridor, she nearly ran into Captain Cullen.

"Pardon me, Ms. Rin," Cullen said.

Ayla deftly sidestepped to get out of the way of him, stopping to greet him. "Good afternoon, Captain. Is everything going well with the ship?"

He gave her a small smile. "Truth be told, the ship runs itself once the course is set in, and we're on our way. We have to have someone monitoring to ensure nothing goes wrong, but it handles all the hyperspace calculations through the computer much better than a human can. Sometimes, the bridge can get pretty boring."

"A war gives you something more meaningful to do then?" Ayla asked, curious about the naval life. Some military men relished in the idea of combat, but she had a feeling the shipmen didn't quite have the same predilection toward action the Marines did.

Cullen glanced at the door leading to Dolman's lab. "I suppose it's better than standard patrols or shakedown runs to make sure the ship's systems are still running. But I signed up for the Imperial Navy in hopes I could explore." He chuckled. "I suppose we're exploring now, too. The *Lyonesse* gets to be one of the first ships to make it out of the galaxy. Or are we the first? I'll have to look into the histories."

"Either way, this is something few humans have ever experienced," Ayla said. "Though, it would be nicer under less strenuous circumstances, yes?"

"That's exactly what I'm getting at." Cullen ran his hand back through his hair. "Say, when you're done, would you be interested in joining me in the captain's quarters for dinner this evening? The chef prepares me a little extra compared to the rest of the crew. You might like the cuisine."

Was he asking her on a date? In the middle of this? She supposed if she called him on it, he would talk about how she's an honored guest or some nonsense and how it's his duty with his station to provide her a pleasant atmosphere and amenities.

Oh, the struggles of being a genetically enhanced female in every regard, from her physique to the pheromones she produced. Men fell for her too easily, which is part of why she'd not ventured into a serious relationship since she'd become an agent.

Still, it *was* getting more than tedious to spend her nights in her quarters studying the Darmarin or trying to avoid the Marines in the mess hall who treated her with disdain out of some misplaced loyalty to Lieutenant Lansing. Cullen also seemed like a nice enough man. What could it hurt?

"I'd be delighted to," Ayla said.

"Great. I'll see you at 1900 hours?" Cullen asked.

"I'll be there."

Cullen gave her a polite nod before turning toward the door. It opened for him, and Dolame's bright voice greeted him from inside.

Ayla couldn't help but smile as she sauntered back down the corridor. With Lansing being so brash toward her, it was nice to have someone treat her with polite interest, at the very least. It would take away from the stresses she felt regarding how dangerous this mission was becoming.

16

Captain Cullen's invitation made for a somewhat awkward situation. He'd set candles, an ornate cloth with several frills on the edge on his table, all set against a full backdrop of the streaking light of hyperspace from a floor-to-ceiling window.

His quarters were spacious, and at least the bedroom was behind a different door, giving it more of a formal atmosphere than going to someone's room.

Ayla waited after Cullen ushered her into the dining area. He had some work to finish before they got to their dinner. With little to do during their travels, Ayla didn't mind spending a few minutes of downtime.

The captain seemed nice enough, but Ayla wasn't sure she wanted to push too far into unprofessional territory. Men often became jittery before battle and wanted companionship, but there was only so much she would do.

It ran contrary to what many people thought of the spy game. In her profession, many imagined promiscuity as the norm to extract information from targets or manipulate political situations.

However, Ayla found she could manage to sway the perception of men with a smile and some small talk when the need arose. Their thoughts of pursuing her often bore a lot of fruit when she needed jobs done.

Even the first time she'd used simple flirting as a tool on a mission, she'd felt guilty about it. Something about manipulating a man's emotions never sat quite right with her, but over time, she became used to it.

She supposed it would be similar to going further with a man, but Ayla had standards she didn't want to become desensitized to.

This wasn't even the first captain in recent memory to show an interest in her. Mihael, the Robeni pirate captain, had been more than captivated by her. She had to admit, he had a bit of a charm. Much different than Captain Cullen, who was clean-cut, an excellent military man, and seemed to run a very organized ship.

By contrast, Mihael was a little more rugged, off the cuff. She found herself missing her last adventure with him and his crew.

But such was the nature of her work. She would be ever the transient, moving from one place to the next until the Imperium deemed it was time for her to enter a desk job or retire. She probably would opt for the latter, not seeing herself able to sit still in the agency building like Jorus did for a living.

After spending some time thinking about it, Ayla decided she would be polite and cordial, cultivate a friendship, stay a reasonable distance away to discourage any physical moves from being made, and call it an evening. Perhaps he would impress her, or maybe he wouldn't, but either way, no commitments would be made, and she could have a clean conscience by treating him well.

Finally, Cullen emerged from the other room. "My apologies for taking so long," he said. "Engineering was registering some anomalies with our stealth systems, and I wanted to make sure we wouldn't have any unforeseen problems as we approach the alien's planetoid."

"Anything I should be worried about?" Ayla asked.

If the ship was going to have technical problems, this would be about the worst time for it to happen. They had already gone far outside of the galaxy. No other humans would be around to rescue them. She might have pirates tailing them, but she couldn't be sure.

Don't let me down, Mihael.

Her thoughts kept returning to the pirate captain while she was with Cullen. She couldn't help but compare them. Both men had taken an interest in her, after all.

"Nothing our team can't handle," Cullen said, giving her a confident smile. There wasn't a trace of doubt behind it either. He respected his crew. That was always a good sign.

He slid over to the table, where he'd had some clay dishes which had been covered. "I wasn't sure what kind of cuisine you liked, so I took the best of what was given to me for the reserves here. Dry aged steak good for you?"

Ayla thought about when Jorus had taken her to the steakhouse in New Austin. Men loved their red meat, didn't they? She couldn't say she minded it. "I'd be delighted."

The captain motioned to a seat for her, and she graciously took it. At the same time, he prepared the meat, asparagus, and brown rice to accompany the steak—a healthy meal, all things considered, and much better than anything the crew had in the mess, which mostly was pre-prepared meals made from nutrient packs to mimic natural flavors. They never quite tasted right.

Cullen seated himself, taking a fork and knife into his hand. "Tell me about yourself."

Ayla couldn't help but laugh. "No pressure."

"Apologies. Should I be more specific?"

She shook her head. "No, it's fine. It just makes me think where I should begin. I was a cop on Terra Prime before the Agency recruited me. I think Jorus liked my strong sense of justice and lack of fear in pursuing violent crimes. I had a partner back then, of course. It doesn't generally go well for a fifty-kilogram-sized woman to be going up against hardened criminals alone. I mean, we had weapons and armor, but you know what I mean."

"Sounds like some tough hand-to-hand combat situations. I thought I read you'd been genetically modified?" He cut into his steak and took a bite while asking.

"Yes, though that came after the Agency identified me for the job. No, on the police beat, it was just the good ol' natural me."

She thought back to those days. They'd seemed like the distant past even though it had only been less than five years since she'd come to the Agency. Jorus had been running her ragged.

"Sounds like you've been serving the Imperium your whole life. I have, too, in ways. I come from a long line of fleeters. My uncle got the furthest in recent family history, becoming an X.O. of a vessel. The family was proud when I was given the captaincy."

"I bet they were. You came up through the academy and everything?" Ayla asked.

Cullen nodded. "Even from the Youth Space Navy program. I knew what I wanted from a young age."

"I didn't know what I wanted to do until the middle of college," Ayla said. She remembered university and the myriad classes she'd tried before finally settling on her career path. "It was a forensics course, and the professor set up the labs like we would be investigating into actual mysteries. We were graded on how fast and thoroughly we completed the assignments. It was oddly relaxing to look at evidence, analyze it, and come to conclusions. It prepared me well for what I do now."

"And what are you analyzing about me?" Cullen brandished quite a smile. It was charming, albeit misplaced.

"That you're trying too hard," Ayla said. She winked to soften the blow, not wanting to upset the captain. He needed to calm down about her, though. The way he leaned over the table and kept fidgeting with the food, he had all the signs of nervous flirting that others might not consciously notice. However, Ayla had a lot of experience in analyzing behavior patterns.

His eyes darkened, and the smile dropped rather quickly. Cullen didn't seem to register her wink at first or that she was mostly playful —even though she wanted to have him back down. He grabbed a glass nearby, pouring wine into it and holding it up. "Just a friendly meeting, then?"

"You got it. Sorry if I gave another impression," Ayla said.

Cullen laughed. "No, no. A man can hope, though, yeah? I just wanted to have a relaxing evening with someone pleasant—and pleasant to look at," He dipped his head toward her with the latter statement.

"The compliment is appreciated. You're a handsome man yourself," Ayla said. Some men took rejection better than others, to Cullen's benefit. It made her respect him more. "But let's have a nice evening, yes?"

She moved to cut her steak, taking a bite soon after. It wasn't top-tier restaurant quality like Jorus liked to take her to, but the food still was tasty, and the meat hadn't dried out in the preparation, which was difficult to attain on long voyages like this one. She'd been in first-class cabins of starliners with worse food.

"Of course. Liking the food?"

"It's enjoyable," Ayla said. "I appreciate you getting me out of the mess with the Marines."

Cullen chuckled. "The ground-pounders. They're quite the lot. Lansing's cultivated a tight-knit group. I have to give him that. I should probably do a little more with my crew."

"We can learn from each other."

"But he's quite the work, isn't he? Seems to view everyone as a target or enemy. And poor Dr. Dolame! I swear he's going to make her break down into tears."

It was Ayla's turn to laugh. She wasn't the only one who noticed how Lansing's behavior impacted others. The Marine meant well, but he came off as abrasive and angry a lot of the time. "I've done my best to shield her from the impact, but he sure does have a way with words. He hasn't exactly been the kindest to me either."

Cullen frowned. "Do you need me to talk to him?"

Ayla waved off the suggestion. "No, no. I can handle myself. Thank you, though. It's sweet." She looked out the window into hyperspace. "I don't think he's a bad person, but just very myopic. There's more at play here than just him and his men. He almost briefly opened up to me about the very concept of aliens bothering him."

Silence hung in the air for a moment, the captain setting down his knife. "I have to admit, learning about sentient alien life unsettles me as well."

"It exists. There's nothing we can do to put the Darmarin back in Pandora's box."

"I suppose you're right. And I can read the room here, at least in that I'm fifty percent of it. Maybe we should talk about something else?"

Ayla let out another light laugh. "Good suggestion. Seen any good holos lately?"

17

"APPROACHING THE DARMARIN PLANETOID," LIEUTENANT JG CETERA said, tapping the controls to his helm station.

Captain Cullen leaned forward in his chair. He seemed to have a habit of such when something excited him. "All hands prepare for engagement. Is our stealth drive working properly?"

Ensign Douglas spoke through the comm from engineering. "All running according to specs."

Ayla stood on the bridge with Lansing, Parello, and Dolame, watching the *Lyonesse* drop from hyperspace into the dark between galaxies. There didn't seem to be the bright light of stars around, which could be seen at nearly all times when they were in the Milky Way—a tapestry of beautiful light she missed about now. It left her feeling empty, like something was taken from her—a full separation from creation.

"This is what hell must be like," Lansing said, echoing her fears. When the Marine got religious, he seemed much more human.

Ayla thought about suggesting he keep his focus on God, but she didn't want to say anything that might be construed as negative during this tense situation.

Parello had an earpiece in as he sat at the conn, listening and paying attention to the various frequencies transmitted around. "I don't hear any chatter on any of the frequencies our AI determined the Darmarin used from our trip to their ship. Everything's dead quiet."

"Hmm," Captain Cullen said. "Quiet is good because it means they're not talking about our arrival here. It also makes me nervous. Any other signs of activity from the planetoid?"

The scanners created an image of the planetoid on the screen based on a compilation of different signatures. It was as close of an approximation to a camera as one could get, and only a trained eye could spot the difference.

Then, multiple points of bright red light appeared on the screen.

"What's that?" Lansing asked.

Parello tapped on his control panel. "It's a heat signature coming from the sensors. It looks like multiple items are being launched from the planetoid."

"Can we identify the objects?" Captain Cullen asked.

"Awaiting data," Parello said, focused on his task. Then, he looked up toward the captain. "They appear to be a series of drones, and they're headed toward us."

"They know we're here," Lansing grumbled. His face went flat. His tone had the air of a man who wanted to say, "I told you so," but was also too proud to state it.

Ayla agreed with Lansing that this was a dangerous situation. The Darmarin knew they were coming, but they still had to continue their mission. Aliens supporting an insurrection needed to be interrupted somehow, and this was all the Imperium could do for the time being.

"Disengage our stealth mode and activate our defensive shielding," Cullen said. "Helm, set a course so our forward lasers keep the drones within our targeting rage."

"Aye, sir," both Parello and Cetera said in unison.

"Lansing, take over tactical," Cullen said.

Lieutenant Lansing made his way to the console, not putting up any argument now that they were about to be in the heat of battle.

Ayla had to stand by and be an observer. She understood her role while coming aboard. It was the problem with her being outside the military system.

Even though she didn't like being helpless to do anything but watch, unable to assist the men as they prepared for a space battle, she kept quiet so as not to distract them.

Anything she said would only slow down their reaction times, which they couldn't afford. They had to get past this drone onslaught and make it to the planetoid before she could be of any help.

The drones came closer, but according to the tactical map, which now overlaid the main screen with Lansing putting it up for all to see, they were still out of firing range. The waiting made things excruciating, and the silence of the bridge was painful to endure.

"Firing range in five, four, three…" Lansing said, keeping his eyes trained on his console.

"Hold steady," Captain Cullen said.

"…two, one."

"Fire! Helm, engage evasive maneuvers."

Lansing furiously hit the controls to engage the ship's lasers, while Cetera brought the ship into a movement pattern that almost appeared random.

The drones continued forward. Dozens of them came into range and began opening fire upon the ship in return. Laser blasts filled space outside, with several drones getting hit and becoming debris.

The ship took return fire, the drones blasting into the energy shielding.

"Shields holding at seventy percent," Lansing said as he worked his magic on the console.

"Good work. Keep at the drones."

A second wave of drones approached the ship, blasting their way like the previous ones. Lansing did all he could to keep up with the assault, but some of the drones came within too close range of the ship for the lasers to be effective.

This is where it would be helpful to have a fighter squadron or drones of their own, but the *Lyonesse* was a smaller ship than many of the Imperial warships. It didn't have any of those defenses. It was meant for stealth and covert missions. Unfortunately, they were now in a full-frontal assault.

The ship rocked.

"Report," Captain Cullen said, swinging his head toward Parello.

"Several of the drones got through our defense shielding. They've jammed themselves into the hull, penetrating decks four, seven, and nine forward," Parello said.

"Engineering, you there?"

"On the comm, Cap'n," Douglas said.

"Can you get those things out of my ship before they do real damage?"

"Trying, but they've wedged themselves in perfectly to where they're using the compression to..." He paused.

"There's a gaseous mixture coming through the areas where the drones have penetrated, Captain," Parello said.

Cullen stood. "Seal the areas. We have to protect against potential poisons."

These Darmarin were dangerous. Since they weren't human, they didn't seem to follow the same rules of warfare that the Imperium did. Not that the Imperium had faced real war in hundreds of years, but at that point, there was some kind of decorum around what would be acceptable or not.

Even the device Ayla had recently preserved from falling into the Scorpio Alliance's hands would be deemed too terrible to actually use —destroying whole planets to settle conflicts was uncivilized. Such things had been used before, and too much loss of life resulted.

But the emperor commanded the remaining device anyway, and it was safe now with two keys held apart to prevent it from being deployed.

With aliens, however, all bets would be off. What kind of morals did the Darmarin even have? Dolame posited they had some sort of resource problem based on what they'd seen of their ship, but it was only a theory. They needed more information on the creatures.

For now, they seemed to have no qualms about poisoning the atmosphere of their enemies.

"I've got it sealed," Douglas said through the comm. "Working on a way to get the drones extracted from our hull. Part of their being wedged in is because of the pressurization of the area. If I can exhaust the remaining air, it will have the side effect of removing all the poison from the areas. In theory, it will also jettison the drones."

"Do it," Cullen said.

A few moments passed, and the drone-affected areas appeared on a tactical map overlay on the screen, which showed the front of the ship. The drones flashed red on the display, and a bar appeared, showing the atmosphere drained from the area. It started slowly and sped up as the air dissipated.

"Agh, I made a mistake," the engineer said through the comm. "I need *more* pressure to push them out, not less."

"You're thinking on the fly," Cullen said.

As this transpired, Lansing kept working on targeting the other drone before the *Lyonesse*. Some fired lasers back, and it seemed like this entire array was sent to try to soften the ship up. For what, Ayla could only brace herself.

The wedged drones blasted out from the ship.

"Reverse. Get us in range to fire at them," Cullen said.

Cetera tapped at the helm controls, moving the ship to thrust in reverse. With the drones having to deal with the pressure situation, they had not recalibrated in time to move on their own as of yet, and Parello was able to blast them out of space.

"Three more left," Cullen said, tracking them on the screen.

Cetera maneuvered the ship to get Lansing the best possible line of sight for his shots, and Lansing expertly used the lasers to take care of the final three drones.

The captain fell back into his seat, letting out a deep breath. "Great job everyone. Round one with these Darmarin goes to the humans."

"Let's hope round two isn't something we can't handle on our own," Lansing said, his regular grumpiness returning.

Even if it didn't boost morale, the lieutenant was right about a lot. And regardless of what the aliens sent at them next, the *Lyonesse* could only take so much of a beating before they'd be stranded and dead in space.

18

AFTER THE DRONES HAD BEEN DESTROYED, NO ONE SPOKE ON THE bridge for a time. Even though it had been hectic, the hull pierced, and areas filled with poisoned gasses, they had gotten out of the onslaught relatively unscathed—no more drones approached the ship, nor any manned vessels. Everything seemed quiet in front of the asteroid.

It scared Ayla.

If the Darmarin knew they were coming, why would they be so quiet about everything? There were defenses, but surely an alien species that was waging a war across galaxies could put up something more of a defense.

Ayla had been in the pirate vessel when humanity had first encountered the Darmarin, and it had taken the help of an Imperial warship to be able to thwart the aliens. They weren't unequipped in their fights.

The *Lyonesse* was more in line with the warship than with a pirate vessel, but alone against however many of the Darmarin were out there. It could only do so much.

"Are we going to wait around for the aliens to regroup and come at us with whatever other surprises they have out there?" Lansing asked.

Cullen raised a brow toward the tactical station. "Are you itching for action, Lieutenant? I thought you were trying to get us to turn around and go home."

"We're here now. I don't like the situation, but if we have gotten past the planetoid's defenses, I don't want to squander the opportunity either," Lansing said.

"What do you suggest?"

"We need to get a landing party together quickly. My men and agent Rin," Lansing said.

Ayla crossed her arms over her chest. "Dr. Dolame is going to need to be on this mission. She's the expert, and if we're going to try to extract data about the aliens from this planetoid, she needs to be with us."

Lansing wrinkled his nose, looking like he wanted to argue about it, but he drooped his head in a resigned fashion. "Fine, but you're on babysitter duty. I can only do so much to keep my men safe in this kind of environment."

Cullen clasped his hands together and stood. "I'm glad to see we're all working together like one happy family," he quipped. "You and your Marines are dismissed from the bridge so you can form your away team. Head to the airlock and keep us appraised of what's happening."

"On it, Captain," Lansing said, his tone becoming more formal.

He didn't mess around, but at least Dolame would be included. Ayla tapped her comm.

"Is it time?" Dolame said on the other end.

"It is. You ready?"

"No, but I'll do what I can."

"Don't worry, I've got you," Ayla said, following the Marines as they filed in line to get off the bridge.

They stepped into the elevator, and breaking the silence, Lansing muttered, "Hail Mary, full of grace, the Lord is with thee. Blessed art thou amongst women, and blessed is the fruit of thy womb, Jesus. Holy Mary, mother of God, pray for us sinners, now and at the hour of our death. Amen."

"Amen," Parello echoed.

Ayla glanced at the comms officer. "You're Catholic, too?"

Parello shook his head. "Figured it can't hurt, though. And we sure seem to be fighting demons, don't we?"

She couldn't argue with his logic. They dropped several decks, and the elevator doors opened to let them out. They moved toward the locker room to change into their pressure suits, where Dolame and the other Marines met with them.

"Men, I need you to be careful out there. We've had one encounter with these creatures already, and we know they're crafty and love to set traps. They're also cowards, unable or unwilling to face us directly. We can use that to our advantage," Lansing said, pacing the locker room as his men tightened the straps on their suits and got themselves situated.

Ayla was impressed with Lansing's reasoning skills. He'd gleaned a lot into the aliens based on the encounter, and she had to say, she had a similar thought about the Darmarin.

Her one encounter with them had been a single alien hiding in an encounter suit, pretending to be a human who wanted to influence the course of the world. The whole point had been trying to manipulate a populace into falsifying memories, molding them into the perfect fighting force on their behalf.

The Darmarin didn't like to fight directly. They'd had more than enough confirmation based on their experiences.

"He's right," Ayla said, backing up Lansing.

The Lieutenant inclined his head toward her.

"I've fought them before," Ayla continued, pacing across the room with the men in their suits. "And we've done this before, too. The asteroid we visited as a training mission was much like this one. The brass picked it because it had similar characteristics and size." She exhaled. "What I mean to say is we've all been here before. It's not as new or as frightening as it appears. We've got this."

She didn't know if she was any good at giving inspirational speeches. Most spy games involved private meetings and persuading people through one-on-one interactions.

Her whole line of work meant she didn't often stand in front of a group and give these kinds of morale-boosting talks. But the look of approval in Lansing's eyes told her she had done well.

He clasped his hands together. "Ms. Rin is right. The plan is to thrust toward the planetoid, enter where we can get to the main computer core for Dr. Dolame to download the data, set explosive charges, and get out. Are there any questions before we head out and engage our target?"

"Sir, no, sir!" the Marines said in unison.

They sounded strong, proud, and completely unfazed by the daunting task ahead of them. Lansing had trained his men well, and part of her lamented that she didn't have that sense of camaraderie or brotherhood they did. Oh well, life choices.

Lansing motioned toward the door, and the men filed in individually. Lansing moved behind them, leaving Dolame and Ayla at the back.

Ayla stepped before the doctor. "You ready for this?"

Dolame gave a small, sheepish smile. "You know I'm not, but I'll do what I must."

Ayla patted her on the shoulder. "Let's get the data and ensure you head home safely." She motioned for the other woman to move ahead.

Once everyone left the room, Ayla secured the last straps on her pressure suit and put her helmet on to follow. She would bring up the back of the line, *babysitting* Dolame as Lansing had asked. It wasn't any skin off her back. She liked the doctor, even if the woman wasn't combat-ready.

As they ventured into the corridor, there were no complaints from her. As much as Dolame might have been thrust into a situation out of her comfort zone, she didn't complain.

Truthfully, they all were out of any potential normalcy in this mission. How could anyone be anything but nervous with the prospect of facing aliens outside of the galaxy? She tried not to think about it too hard. She had to deal with the task at hand just like the others.

They reached the airlock. Each of them made one last check on their pressure suits and helmets to ensure their respective atmospheric pressures would hold inside, and then Parello hit the commands to decompress the chamber.

The doors opened a moment later to lights shining off the hull and a pitch-black spacescape behind it. The sight made chills run through Ayla's bones.

All the preparations they'd made evaporated. It dawned on her exactly how far they were out, away from the rest of humanity, isolated, alone in the dark. Judging from the silence from the others' comm units, they had much the same dread.

"Launch," Lansing said, activating the thrusters on his suit. He lifted off the floor plating and moved forward, floating into the vacuum. His Marines followed.

Dolame and Ayla were last to leave the airlock, maneuvering after the Marines toward the planetoid. The suit thrusters gave them some control, but it also had intelligent compensation, which kept them from pushing too hard and ramming into the people in front of them.

Ayla turned her head back to look at the *Lyonesse*. It had taken damage where the drones had assaulted it, with black scuffs on the hull, and as she floated farther from the bay, the areas where the drones had burrowed and penetrated the hull were revealed.

Sparks shot from blown-out conduits, flickering into the force-field at regular intervals. It was an energy drain, but something Douglas would have to deal with in engineering. She could do nothing from her position.

She turned her head back to face the rest of her group. They pressed forward and away from the *Lyonesse*, floating away from the exterior lights of the airlock area and slowly dimming into the darkness toward the planetoid.

"Good luck, people," Captain Cullen said through their comms. "We will be breaking off and making sure the ship is out of range of any possible Darmarin sneak attacks. When you've completed your mission, fire up a beacon, and we'll come to extract you."

"Copy that, Captain," Lansing said.

The *Lyonesse* let off a soft blue glow as its thrusters activated, pushing in the opposite direction of the landing party. The glow faded as the ship moved farther away, leaving Ayla, Dolame, and the Marines in the middle of nothingness.

They headed toward the asteroid at what felt like a snail's pace, the thrusters keeping steady to keep them on their trajectory. The moment of truth about what the Darmarin had in wait for them would be soon.

19

THE THRUST TO THE PLANETOID WENT VERY MUCH LIKE THEIR ASTEROID training mission. How the brass had figured this planetoid would be so similar to the supply depot they used to prepare was beyond Ayla. Scientists and analysts had so many means by which to gather information on a situation that was beyond her understanding.

Even within the mission, the amount of data Dr. Dolame had uncovered on the Darmarin astounded her. The scientist had a cursory understanding of some of the alien language, their culture, and their potential motivations for attacking the Imperium. All from a brief encounter where Ayla barely had gotten out alive.

It's why she didn't take the same hardline position Lansing had. If they could glean even more information about the Darmarin, it would be invaluable to figure out how to fight them and stop them from aiding their enemies.

One could only hope this would pay off. However, that information would never be returned if they didn't make it out of there. At least Dolame could transmit their small amount of data back to Terra Prime.

"Is everyone with me?" Lansing asked through the comm.

The Marines shouted "here" in unison, followed by Dolame and Ayla.

"Good. I see a small area that looks like one of the tubes where the drones launched from. Kleinman, Miller, go on ahead and scout for us to make sure it's clear. Let Olsen know if you need some of these explosives planted to bust a hole in there."

"Yes, sir," Kleinman and Miller said together. The two infantrymen hit their thrusters harder, speeding away from the group closer to the planetoid.

The rest of them waited, breathing into their suits. Space could feel so silent, empty.

"Looks like it's clear. The tube is open and empty from where the drone deployed. Should we go in?" Kleinman asked.

"We're here to infiltrate this planetoid, soldier. Full speed ahead," Lansing said.

One by one, the rest of The Emerald Array followed Kleinman and Miller into the access tube. Ayla and Dolame followed, but Richards brought up the rear.

"Making sure we don't lag behind?" Ayla asked the medic.

"If drones decide to come back into their home base tube here and catch us from behind, I want to make sure our scientist isn't the first in the line of fire," he said.

The words chilled Ayla. With the Darmarin knowing of their arrival, this could have been some elaborate ruse to corral them into one area and snuff them out.

The team sunk inside the access tube, rock mixed with metal supports for the drones to use for launch. It was dark inside, dead, much like the Darmarin ship they'd encountered earlier in their journey.

Perhaps it was more of the energy conservation of resources Dolame had theorized. The more Ayla saw, the more facts seemed to confirm the scientist's theories.

Kleinman overshot his thrust and bounced against the tube wall. He smashed against a metallic strut, which crumbled against his weight. Rock and debris floated in the open space.

Dolame started breathing heavily, gasping for air. She braced herself against one of the side walls and stopped moving forward.

Ayla placed a hand on the woman's shoulder pad. "Are you okay?"

"I'm having trouble breathing. Panic attack. It's claustrophobic in here."

"Well, we have to keep moving. It'll be better once we get inside the area where the aliens live and breathe. They're much larger than us, and their rooms and hallways are bigger," Ayla said.

"I know...it's just..."

One of the loose bars smacked against the other side of the rock wall, causing more to come loose and rocks to fly everywhere. Small pebbles hit Ayla's face mask, but not at high enough speed to do any real damage.

"We can't stay here," Lansing said. "Keep going or we'll expose ourselves to something dangerous."

"I know it's hard," Ayla said. "Try to breathe slowly. In through the nose, out through the mouth." She recalled the medication techniques Jorus had taught her before. "Try to count to four with each breath, hold it, and hold it on the way out again. Trust me, it calms nerves in situations like this."

"That's the same technique I teach my Marines," Lansing said, his voice sounding approving for once.

"The agency uses many of the military tactics we've found to work on our smaller scale. I think we have more in common than you realize," Ayla said.

It was enough to meet with a grunt from the Marine. He didn't like being reminded of their similarities.

The other Marines kept descending into the tube. The fear of collapse was irrational. The worst that could happen would be they'd be trapped there.

The planetoid didn't have any gravity pulling the rocks downward, so they would simply float around until they managed to push their way out. But Ayla knew explaining the situation to Dolame wouldn't do any good.

After a few rounds of the breathing technique, the woman seemed to calm down. "I think I'm good now. Thanks, Ayla."

"No problem."

They all proceeded forward, shining flashlights down to where they found the area where the drones parked. It had a piston spurring mechanism to assist in launch and a harness for the drones for when they weren't activated. There appeared to be a small hatch for the Darmarin to use as an entrance to work on the drones.

Miller pointed to the hatch. "There's our way in. Looks like it's sealed."

Olsen pushed past his teammates. "Good thing I'm here to blast our way in. You know what to do next. Don't get yourself caught in the radius."

The explosives expert had a much larger pack on him than the rest of the crew, which would have been impossible to carry in normal gravity, but he managed it since they were floating around.

He turned and fumbled through it momentarily until he found a small device which he attached to the hatch. Then, he stepped back and commanded the fuse to light using the wrist console on his suit.

The explosion was small and contained, with little force coming back in their direction due to the lack of gravity, but it was enough to blow a hole in the hatch. Air came rushing from inside into the tube as the pressure equalized, and after the initial rush had faded, they all moved inside.

Olsen was first, setting his pack down on the ground in the large compartment area, which appeared to be a drone repair facility given all the spare parts around. No lights were on. There was no moisture or dripping anywhere, common with what they saw in other Darmarin facilities. The creatures had their allergies to water, which is why they seemed to thrive on dead planetoids like this one.

The rest of the Marines dropped to the floor as they came into the gravity. Dolame followed, and Miller helped her to her feet with a less-than-graceful landing. Ayla and Richards brought up the rear.

Once inside, Miller grabbed some sheet metal and a drill from his pack, sealing up the compartment so the air could settle inside and pressurize again.

"Atmosphere is breathable," Parello said, his scanning equipment in hand.

"I'm going to keep my helmet on if it's all the same. I'd recommend we all do. We don't know what we're going to face out here, and the drones the aliens sicced on us already used some form of gas attack on the ship," Lansing said.

"Sounds like a prudent plan," Ayla said. The man had a good knack for making sure his men stayed safe.

They glanced around the area, and Dolame moved to what appeared to be a terminal station. "I wonder how to turn this on."

Parello worked with her, the two toying with different hand commands and eventually getting into the wiring of the terminal as they worked.

Lansing and his other men inspected the drone parts.

"There's enough parts here to handle hundreds of these buggers," Kleinman said.

"The last thing we need is the Scorpio Alliance to get ahold of a drone production facility. Could you imagine?" Miller asked.

"I can," Lansing said, picking up what appeared to be a long antenna. He snapped it in half. "The material they're using is fragile, though. Very thin."

"Dolame's theory is the Darmarin come from a galaxy of extremely limited resources, which is why they're coming after ours," Ayla said, casually walking the floor and glancing at the different compartments full of parts.

"It's a good theory," Lansing said. "Makes as much sense as anything I've seen so far."

Lights flickered on from the console behind them, brightening the room to where shadows fell everywhere from the drone parts. It made it easier to see than their wrist flashlights, though.

Dolame had her computer equipment interfacing with the alien tech. She seemed fully immersed, eventually moving to operate the

Darmarin controls to get the full room lights on. They weren't that much brighter than it was in the dark.

"Hopefully, this helps. From what I can tell, the Darmarin come from an environment of burrowing, much like we see in the planetoid here," Dolame said. "Their eyesight operates better under dark or semi-light conditions, and this is as bright as they need to be able to work."

"Makes for one creepy place," Kleinman said.

"Also perfect for an ambush," Lansing said. "Keep your eyes peeled. They sent out drones, so they are very aware that we're here. I am waiting for the trap to spring."

Something *screeched* in the bowels of the planetoid, followed by a *clank*. It was metallic, and the timing gave Ayla goosebumps after Lansing's words.

"What was that?" Ayla asked.

Lansing raised his laser rifle, powering it up. The battery cartridge glowed in the dim supply bay. "Sounds like the enemy. Be vigilant."

His men similarly readied their weapons. Ayla pulled her laser pistol from its holster, not about to be carrying a heavy rifle like the Marines. She preferred to be more agile in her fighting style. It came with the drawbacks of less armor and firepower but more maneuverability.

Several small drones shot into the room, different from the ones that had attacked the ship. Those had large compartments for their payloads. These had saucer-like tops with several tentacles stretching downward and propellers guiding them on the saucer's top and sides. Six entered in total, and they started blasting with their lasers.

"More drones! These aliens must have a whole fleet of them!" Miller shouted.

The Marines naturally moved for cover, taking up positions among several of the supply compartments. Parello grabbed Dr. Dolame and set himself between her and the drones before pushing her down by the shoulders to hide behind the terminal where she'd been working.

Her equipment still sat on the terminal, gathering data they could use later if they managed to escape this mess.

Ayla found a contraption that looked like it was meant to grab a drone and push it into the launch tube. It provided adequate cover from the enemy lasers and allowed her to sneak her pistol around the side and return fire.

The Marines worked at a quick and efficient speed. They immediately blasted two of the drones out of the air, the second crashing into a third, which got caught in its propulsion, causing it to smash against a wall, rendering it inoperable.

Three drones would be easy enough target practice for their group. It looked like the Darmarin had no resources to expend upon them.

Ayla trained her laser pistol carefully, aiming for the fourth drone to blast three shots into it, knocking it to the floor as well.

The fifth one came close, shooting at Miller and hitting him in his pressure suit's arm. However, Lansing was right there to raise the butt of his laser rifle and jam it into the drone's propellers, crushing the device against the wall.

The Marines focused fire on the last drone, barraging it with the sum of their laser rifle capabilities. It shattered and hit the floor a moment later.

"Everyone in one piece?" Lansing asked. He moved over to Miller, who cradled his arm. "How are you doing over there?

"It clipped me. The suit's filler auto-patched the hole, so I'll be all right. Arm stings but got a painkiller spray deployed," Miller said.

"Glad it wasn't serious." Lansing looked to the area ahead where the drones had come from. "Their defenses are much lighter than I anticipated, given their advanced knowledge of our arrival. Something smells about all of this."

"Regardless, it looks like we'll be able to complete our mission," Ayla said, maneuvering herself toward the alien console to check on Dolame.

The scientist eased herself back up, glancing at her equipment on the terminal. Parello stood with her, vigilantly guarding her. As much as Lansing had said the Marines wouldn't be babysitting her, it appeared the computer expert understood her value.

"All of my equipment looks okay. Nothing took any hits in the crossfire," Dolame said, tapping at some of the controls. "I've uploaded almost everything here in the databanks. We'll have a full spectrum of their language and whatever historical data is contained here within the hour. I can start piecing together the purpose of the base here soon with the help of our AI."

"Excellent," Lansing said. "Let's clear this place and see if we can find anything else of use. Marines, attention!"

The men stood at attention.

"Forward, march," Lansing said.

His men complied, marching deeper into the planetoid, none questioning what may be lurking in its depths to harm them.

20

THE EMERALD ARRAY'S MARCH SLOWED ONCE MORE AS THE DARKNESS enveloped them. They had their wrist flashlights back on, moving slowly ahead into the bowels of the planetoid.

On their way, they found what appeared to be some living quarters, and they stopped at what Dolame said was an intergalactic communications hub.

She used her instruments to gather more data from there, ascertaining that, indeed, this planetoid acted as a bridge point for the Darmarin to stop, gather their resources, and rest before coming into the Milky Way.

This base served as a communications point from the Darmarin already in the humans' galaxy, returning signals to Andromeda.

Dolame went through some of the transmission logs. "Apparently, they've been communicating with multiple systems within Andromeda. I'm trying to gather video. Some of what we've found is transmitted in a different language altogether from Darmarin, which uses different growling sounds at various pitches to communicate. It's pretty fascinating and sounds like singing, in a way."

She had an earpiece against her head where she listened, but no one else could hear the broadcasts.

"Fascinating," Lansing said, with a tinge of sarcasm in his voice. "Is there any indication of how many forces they have here?" He was always focused on the here and now and what threats might be occurring. It was comforting to have someone so good at protecting along with them.

"I am uncertain on the number of Darmarin potentially here, as this panel seems to be relegated to drone repair and programming," Dolame said, tapping the controls on the alien console. "However, it appears they have nearly a hundred drones in all. I'm not sure if this means different kinds of bots to perform different functions or attack drones."

"One hundred?" Lansing raised his voice with concern.

"That's right."

"We're in trouble. These first volleys were just testing our capabilities. Contact the ship," Lansing said, clutching his laser rifle a little more tightly.

Parello worked on his communication circuit with his wrist control. "Nothing. We're being jammed."

"I knew this would be a trap. Establish a perimeter as best you can. Guard the launch tube. They might use it to send drones this way," Lansing said.

Ayla stepped back to allow Kleinman to guard one entrance and Miller to take a position the way they'd come in.

Miller backpedaled nearly immediately upon arriving where he did. "Lieutenant, we need to fall back deeper into the planetoid."

"What? Why?"

In answer, several drones flooded in from the launch tube. The first assault hadn't been the full capabilities of the Darmarin after all.

"Fall back!" Lansing shouted, training his laser rifle at the enemy targets while shuffling backward toward the interior corridor.

The Marines fell in with him, a barrage of laser fire coming from both directions. Ayla grabbed Dolame by the wrist and pulled her toward the aperture, where the Marines laid cover fire along the way.

"Ow!" Dolame said, but it was her only protest. She accompanied Ayla, and soon they were out into the corridor.

The group moved well together, the Marines covering the women and firing behind them as they descended further into the planetoid. Ayla got the sense they were being herded, but there were too many drones coming from where they had entered for them to stand and fight.

"We have to find a choke point like a door to hold them off," Lansing said.

"Hopefully, there is one," Miller said.

Laser fire continued, filling the air with bright light, followed by dust, creating a smoky atmosphere.

"We could try to cave the ceiling in," Parello said.

It might have been a good idea, but one of the drones pushed forward, moving straight for where Kleinman held the line. The drone lifted its tendrils, locked them into place, and rammed into Kleinman with its tendrils acting as spears.

The metal jammed right through the Marine's armor, causing him to let out a cry of distress that only lasted until the drone had punctured his lungs. The tendrils cut through his entire body, and soon, the Marine fell limp to the ground—the first casualty in their mission.

"Fall back!" Lansing shouted, his voice having more urgency than before.

It was the first time Ayla could recall hearing him afraid.

The group moved much more quickly down the corridor, which sank in elevation into the planetoid in a steep incline. Eventually, they came to an end, where the room opened into something bigger rather than smaller, making for more points for the drones to flood into—the opposite of cover.

In the room was the glow of a power facility. It would have been something worth Dolame studying if they hadn't been too occupied firing their laser weapons to hold off the approaching drones.

The Marines fell into place in front of Ayla and Dolame, all the same, masculine chivalry winning the day, and they would put themselves in a position to die first before the drones could get to the women.

Dolame tapped her wrist comm. "I'm unable to contact the *Peregrine*. We're still being jammed."

"If worse comes to worst," Lansing said, eyes flicking to Ayla for a moment while he continued his suppression fire down the corridor, "use our bodies as shields."

Ayla held up her laser pistol to do her part in keeping the drones off them, depressing the trigger and holding it for a continuous group of laser blasts. "I'll be taking down as many of these things as I can along with you if it comes to it."

Lansing grunted, which seemed to be in some form of respect. Who knew what the Marine meant by it?

But as they stood there in front of the alien power reactor, it became apparent the drones hadn't been pursuing in following them down. They were alone, firing into the near-dark of the corridor and wasting their energies doing so.

"Hold your fire," Lansing commanded.

The Marines obeyed. The dust in the air settled as matters quieted. Where were the drones?

"You've made it very far, humans," a booming, deep voice resounded from the corridor, echoing into the room.

The humans looked at each other, confused.

Dolame was the first to speak, "A Darmarin. I recognize the burr in its vocal patterns that makes it distinct from humans. They don't have the same windpipes or vocal cords we do."

"Astute observation," the voice said, still nobody coming into sight to accompany it. The sheer coldness with which the creature spoke sent shivers down Ayla's spine.

"Show yourself and end this cowardice," Lansing said sternly.

"Not as of yet," the Darmarin said. "I'm sending my drones in to collect your weapons. You will deposit them, or you will be killed. I have dozens more to send through, so you had best not consider any trickery."

Drones flew into the room, and then, at least ten of them, the black metal clogged the airways and gave the place a sudden claustrophobic atmosphere. The closest drones carried small bins for the depositing of weapons.

Lansing moved forward first to put his weapon down, signaling his men to do the same. He didn't hesitate in the matter. They weren't in a situation where they could blast their way out of here anyway, so what good would the weapons do? There was no sense in going down in a blaze of glory, losing the data they'd collected.

"My instruments," Dolame said then in a private helm comm channel to Ayla.

"We can't concern ourselves with them now," Ayla said. They might not ever retrieve them, depending on how this went.

"I wonder," the Darmarin said, "why humanity would send such a small force so easily capturable toward us? Did your masters not realize this would be a suicide mission? Do they value your lives so little?"

The Marines didn't answer the creature, nor would Ayla or Dolame. Whatever this Darmarin thought he could gain by making them distrust their leadership wouldn't work. They were far too well-trained.

The talking helped delay the drones taking weapons off the team, however. Stripped of their potential threats, the humans stood glancing between one another, hoping for a reprieve while the drones backed away.

The room had very little except the power core and subsequent control panels. Ventilation was done through small slits in the ceiling rather than offering any sort of shafts to escape to. They were truly trapped, and there didn't seem to be any hope of a way out.

From the inclined entrance, a Darmarin finally walked down toward them. The creature stood over a head taller than Lansing—the tallest among the group—skinny and lanky, with its body looking more like a shell rather than skin.

It made sense that a creature with a severe allergy to water would present as hardened and dry. It had beady eyes, spikes on its head, and arms that looked more like they should be on a mantis or a crab than a person.

Even though the Marines had seen the Darmarin in images generated from the carcass of the one Dr. Dolame had dissected, they
gasped at the sight of one of their alien enemies in person.

The prospect of encountering intelligent life couldn't help but be
shocking. Ayla recalled her first encounter with one of these creatures, also on a small asteroid base, and her fight leading to its even-
tual demise.

She hadn't exactly been scared, but it was uncomfortable, and at
the time, not knowing the alien's weakness, she had no idea if she
would make it out alive.

This situation seemed worse.

They were too far off to call for help. The ship couldn't even hear
them in here. If one of them could get to the exterior of the planetoid,
it might be possible to contact them to get the *Lyonesse* involved in the
fight. But even if they arrived, what could they do? Blow up the place?

Ayla supposed it would be better to take the Darmarin down with
them than allow them to continue with this base of operations. It
wasn't the way she wanted to meet her end, however.

"I don't fear you, demon," Lansing said suddenly, bringing Ayla out
of her thoughts.

The Darmarin stepped toward Lansing, peering down over him.
"You realize I am in a position to end your life at my command?"

"Death holds no sting for me," Lansing replied.

Ayla had heard similar words before. Where did they come from?
She struggled to recall, but it sounded like it had a religious connota-
tion. It must be nice to have such assurance.

The Darmarin seemed perplexed by Lansing's proclamation,
staring at the Marine for a long moment. "You humans are strange
creatures. I can't presume to understand. But I don't need to. I merely
need to eradicate your existence from the galaxy."

"Why do you feel the need to do this?" Dr. Dolame asked. She was
probing for information on the Darmarin, keeping her wits even in
this difficult situation where they faced certain death from the alien's
drones.

"The Andromeda Galaxy has races much older than the mere

millennia humans have expanded across the Milky Way," the Darmarin said, pacing in front of the group. "I'm sure you've ascertained from the data you've collected on my people so far that our galactic home is sparse on resources. Over the millennia, our worlds have been depleted of its metallic deposits, and we seek to replenish them. The Milky Way, by contrast, is rich in resources."

"Why not just open trade?" Dolame asked.

"You presume we have something with which you would value. Perhaps there are technologies your people have not yet discovered, but it would be a one-time trade, and soon, we would have nothing to offer. Our great hive-mind has already run calculations on every possible scenario you might be able to conceive." The Darmarin spoke flatly, with little to no emotion in what he said. He believed this was a fact, and there was no way forward but war with the Imperium.

Ayla didn't care why they were doing what they were doing. The aliens posed a threat to human life, and it became her duty to eradicate that threat.

Dolame shook her head in disbelief. "Surely we can try some form of diplomacy."

"It's not our mission," Lansing said sternly.

The civilian doctor's face tightened. "I didn't ask you, Lieutenant."

The Darmarin stopped its pacing, inclining its scaly head. "And as you see, the human propensity to fight amongst your own kind is what will eventually be your undoing. We have already exploited this, and it is just the beginning. I hope this knowledge of the superior race bringing about your demise brings you peace in whatever afterlife you believe in."

"If you don't want to talk, why did you bring us here?" Dolame pleaded, getting in front of the larger creature and showing no fear of him in the process.

"Do you earnestly believe you're the only ones on a mission to gather data? How quaint. Again, it will be your egocentric natures and individualism which will lead to your undoing."

The Darmarin turned to walk up the other way.

They were still trapped here, unable to make any path to escape with the drones in the way, and now weaponless. Ayla couldn't even think of how to devise a plan that would work for them. She glanced at Lansing.

The Marine simply shook his head at her. There was no way out of here. Even if they attacked the Darmarin, it would do no good. Even the small information they had learned about his so-called hive mind would be lost because only they heard it, and they had no way to transmit the information back to the *Lyonesse*.

"Dolame," Ayla said.

"Yes?"

"Did you upload what you found when we entered the ship's databanks?" Ayla asked.

"Of course."

Then, their mission, at least, hadn't been entirely for naught. It gave Ayla some sense of peace to know their sacrifice wouldn't be in vain so long as the ship made it out of this darkness between galaxies.

"Drones, dispose of them," the Darmarin said as the creature moved out of view, and the Darmarin's cold, metallic death-dealers hovered ever closer to make their kills.

21

THE DRONES TURNED, LEVELING THEIR LASERS TOWARD THE GROUP. Ayla tensed, ready to drop to the floor and try to evade these blasts, but where could they go?

Miller positioned himself at the front, ready to take blasts before anyone else in the group, but it wouldn't make any difference once they fell. They would all face the laser fire of far too many drones, and though their pressure suits would protect them to some degree, it would be a matter of time before they all took too much damage. They had no shielding, no weapons to return fire. It was hopeless.

Ayla quickly scanned to find some vent, grate, or ladder somewhere, but there was nothing. The power core was behind some kind of plexiglass plating, which didn't allow anyone to go through, and even if they could get back there, the radiation would melt through them before they could get anywhere else within the planetoid.

She didn't want to give up. The drones seemed to give them a long moment to ponder their despair, perhaps some intentional design from the Darmarin to analyze how humans reacted with their literal backs against the wall.

"Marines, charge and take some of them out before they do us in!" Lansing shouted. "Lord, protect us and bring us into Heaven!"

The lieutenant's faith came through in his final moment. He didn't seem afraid at all. He charged forward past Miller, jumping toward one of the drones and grabbing it, then slamming it to the ground as hard as possible. His reaction was so savage, so raw, it startled Ayla.

The other Marines joined in, crying out with guttural yells as they moved forward and took on their own drones, leaving Ayla and Dolame behind to look at each other perplexed.

Ayla didn't wait long as the drones began firing on them. With her genetically enhanced reflexes, she could dodge the opening volleys. "Duck behind the control panel and stay there!" Ayla shouted to Dolame.

The scientist followed orders very well, hiding from view and allowing Ayla to focus on something other than protecting her.

A drone lunged forward with its tendrils, striking between Ayla's arm and side, barely giving her time to get out of the way. Fortunately, the drone didn't manage to scratch her pressure suit.

Ayla turned and grabbed the drone by the tendrils, pulling it down and turning it to force its laser fire into one of the others. The drone receiving the laser blast exploded.

Even though the initial volley had gone well, the humans had the element of surprise against the drones. That element would evaporate within moments. Then, they would truly be out of options.

Miller had taken out three drones by himself in his rampage, but the act had left him out in the middle of the room, completely exposed. Several other drones trained their lasers on him, blasting him together.

The several shots caused him to stagger, convulse multiple times in shock, and collapse to the floor, burnt to a crisp.

Lansing was too caught up in fighting drones to notice his other infantryman go down. He had taken one of the long tendrils from a destroyed drone and was using it like a stick, swinging at others, getting their propellers jammed, and pushing them into more drones.

Regardless of how well they fought, too many drones loomed over them to keep this up forever. Eventually, they would tire, and the war of attrition would not be friendly toward the Marines or Ayla.

All they needed in reality, as morose as the thought was, was for one of them to survive. If a single person carried some of the information they discovered through their helmet cams back to the *Lyonesse*, it might have been worth it for them to have gone on this suicide mission.

Dolame would be the one who would preferably survive, but Ayla had to find some way out for her. Even if she managed to escape down the corridor, how would the woman get back to the ship alone?

Her planning of various escape scenarios distracted her in the battle against the drones, the much more pressing problem. The drones struck at her, pelting her pressure suit with lasers.

Fortunately, the armor absorbed the blasts she took before she maneuvered out of the way, dodging the next several shots the drones fired.

She couldn't keep this up forever. Something had to give, and she hoped it wouldn't be her life.

One drone seemed to have her in its sights. It followed her no matter how she dodged its blasts, becoming more than an annoyance. The drone swooped in, jamming its tendrils toward her.

Ayla slammed her forearm to the side, pushing the tendrils away from her body so they wouldn't ram through her. It hurt hitting the metal so hard, but it was better than the alternative of being impaled.

The drone spun in response, throwing her off balance. Ayla lost her footing, slipping and falling onto her rear end.

Three drones honed in on her, two coming at her from each side and the other from directly on top of her. They trained their lasers. This would be it, the end of Ayla's life. She gasped for air even though she had no problem breathing before this.

The moment came too real, too fast, and even though it had been hopeless for a while, it hadn't felt so real or imminent until now.

She squeezed her eyes closed, prepared for her inevitable doom.

Laser shots fired in rapid succession.

Ayla took a breath. She lived. What just happened?

Her eyes fluttered open. The drones surrounding her crashed to the floor, powerless, no longer threats to her existence.

JON DEL ARROZ

Jannik, Rams, and Lycia charged in, laser rifles firing haphazardly.

"Yahoooo!" Jannik said. The young, lanky pirate shouted, his blond hair falling into his face.

Ayla pushed herself back onto her feet. The pirates had arrived. Her friends had come for her and made it at the right moment.

"Got any more weapons?" Ayla asked as Lycia approached her, protecting her from the drones' attacks.

"I'm just a chef. I barely can operate one of these things," Lycia said, offering her laser rifle to Ayla.

She took it into her hands, clutching it tightly as it was more than reassuring to be able to have a weapon. "Thank you."

Not wasting any more time, Ayla started firing. With her training and her genetic modifications, she was able to track the drones and shoot them down far faster than the pirates, but their surprise attack helped them to be able to get the drones off guard and tip the balance of the battle in their favor.

The Darmarin trudged back down the ramp into the bay, visibly angry at what transpired. The creature lashed out toward the pirates, charging Jannik.

"No. No. NO! I accounted for every variable, every contingency. This can't be happening."

Jannik fired his laser rifle at the alien, which had no effect. The young man tightened his lips, sweat dripping down his brow as the sight of the alien made him nervous.

The Darmarin grabbed Jannik by the throat, lifting him off the ground. The lanky man pedaled in the air, trying to get his footing to no avail. He dropped his laser rifle, choking from the Darmarin's grip.

Mihael, the pirate captain, bounded down the ramp, pummeling at full speed into the Darmarin and knocking him off his balance. The alien released Jannik, dropping him to the ground, reeling and spinning toward the pirate captain.

"You'll wish you hadn't done that," the Darmarin said.

"You'll wish you never messed with my crew," Mihael said. He drew his laser pistol and fired a succession of point-blank shots into the alien. Still, the bolts had no effect, simmering into nothingness as the Darmarin stood there unfazed.

The Darmarin, with his hard, shell-like claw, backhanded Mihael across the face, sending the pirate to the floor to join Jannik. They got up very slowly as the battle transpired all around them.

Ayla tried to reach the pirates, her heart leaping joyfully to see Mihael. Did she have some kind of feelings for the pirate captain? He had shown interest in her when she had been aboard her ship, but so had many men. This one was different, however.

He came to her rescue when she needed it, all the way out into the black between galaxies. It brought her some joy, but she would have to consider the implications of his being here later.

For now, she had to face off against drones. She fired several shots into one close to her, dodging under the tendrils of a second to make her way over to the pirates.

"Don't waste the energy. Weapons do no good against the aliens!" she shouted.

"I figured as much," Mihael said wryly as he returned to his feet. He woozily lifted his fists like he was going to punch the creature.

It would also be pointless, as he'd only likely break his knuckles by punching the Darmarin straight on. The creature had a hard shell-like structure, which made it impervious to that kind of attack.

But Ayla knew its weakness—water. There wasn't time to explain it to the pirates as the Darmarin would be jamming its pincer hands into Mihael's belly if the pirate captain made a few more steps forward to get into range. It wouldn't go well for him.

It was up to her to react quickly.

Inside her pressure suit was a tube that carried a pouch of water. She only needed to make it spray toward the alien.

Ayla burst into a run, moving for the Darmarin. With one hand, she tried to loosen the tube from her suit and get it so she could aim air at the creature. It was easier said than done as it was firmly attached. Finally, she yanked it free and slid to a stop between the alien and Mihael.

The Darmarin's features were sterner than humans on average, and his beady eyes stared at her incredulously. "You think you can hurt me? After these larger, stronger beings attempted to attack me and go nowhere?"

"Yes, but I have something they don't," Ayla said.

"What's that?" The Darmarin paused, almost as if her words confused him.

The moment gave her an opening, one she used to turn the end of the tube toward the alien creature. She jammed her other fist into the area of her suit where the water pouch would be, to the left side of her abdomen. The pressure pushed the water up through the channel and shot out of the tube like a gun, splashing directly into the Darmarin's face.

The alien's rocky face fizzled, bubbling with smoke pluming from it. The hard surface melted, its skin—if one could call it skin—dripping down like tears. The alien reached its claws toward its face and howled in desperate pain.

"Everyone, pull the tubes from the compartment in your suit and spray water on the creature. They're deathly allergic," Ayla said.

Mihael reached into his suit and did the same as her, blasting the Darmarin with water again. A couple of his pirates joined him. Even Dr. Dolame came forward from her place of hiding to join in.

"I think I can help here," she said. It was easy for her since the Darmarin already cowered, writhing and reeling as the water kept hitting him—his face, his body, it all melted from the touch of the simple liquid.

Dolame's blast of water finished the alien creature. For all its smug talk during their encounter, a simple amount of what sustained humans in life made it impossible for him to even plea for his life when it came to it. All that came out were more cries before they finally ceased, and the Darmarin died.

The rest of The Emerald Array still fought with drones around them. The pirates had mowed through quite a few of them, and the drones had no sentience. They couldn't understand there was another threat coming, but there was still clean-up work to do.

However, the danger had passed. Ayla reunited with her pirate crew. She turned to Mihael, face to face with the pirate captain.

"Miss me?" Mihael grinned at her.

Ayla brought him into a tight embrace. "More than you know. Let's get out of here and catch up!"

22

THE BATTLE TOOK NEARLY AN HOUR FOR THE MARINES AND THE PIRATES to make it out. Dolame was able to pick up her equipment, which managed to gather a large amount of information on the Darmarin through the facility, and they headed back to their ships.

On the way, Ayla broke it to the Marines. She would be going onto the pirate ship not the *Lyonesse*, but she promised to return soon.

Once inside the familiar airlock of the *Peregrine*, she removed her helmet. Jannik stood beside her, smiling goofily.

"Thought we'd never see you again," the lanky man said.

Rams also removed his helmet and wiped the sweat from his brow. "I hoped we wouldn't. I couldn't see anything profitable about heading this far out into space. It's not like we have promises from the emperor that he'll pay us this round."

His words were meant to guilt Ayla. The pirate wanted assurances they would get compensated once more for their service to the Imperium. What had Mihael promised them when he brought them out here? It wasn't her problem, but she felt terrible for the pirate captain, who she knew took this dangerous trip on for the sake of her.

It was endearing, she had to admit, and it made her feel obligated to help him. But for now, she couldn't make any promises on delivering resources from the Imperium.

"With aliens threatening all of humanity, you've probably just saved your little corner of the galaxy if the information Dr. Dolame brings back can be deciphered," Ayla said.

"That's a big if," Rams replied. "Anyway, I'm glad you seem to be doing well."

"Likewise."

The other pirates greeted her in kind, and Ayla noted a couple of additions to the crew. They'd been doing well for themselves since she'd left. They should be since she was able to get them paid fairly handsomely from the agency coffers the last time she'd met with them.

Allying with Robeni pirates had never been something she'd considered possible, but these were unique times.

They met in the main lounge once they had all settled and gotten out of their pressure suits. Lycia had cooked up some kind of stew that smelled delightful, and she poured small bowls of her concoction to feed her fellow crew.

Mihael entered, his eyes falling hard upon Ayla the moment he arrived, not leaving her. They had a haunting, pining quality to them. The man was strong, though, and he wouldn't beg nor make a fool of himself in front of the rest of the crew.

"You came a long way just to get yourself into trouble with aliens again," the pirate captain said, his lips twitching upward into a tiny smile.

"I go where I'm ordered." She shrugged.

Mihael grabbed his bowl of stew, bringing a spoon to his mouth and blowing on the food to allow it to cool. He then took a ginger bite of it. "Tastes good, Lycia," he said.

"Thanks," Lycia replied while cleaning some dishes behind her counter.

"What's the latest on alien invasion?" Mihael asked.

"Well, we know they're coming to our galaxy because they're out of resources in theirs," Ayla said. "It seems like they plan to have humanity grind each other into dust so they can come in and not have to expend any of their own population on a greater war."

"Great." Mihael's tone came across as very sarcastic. "And with the way things are going, having a talk to unite everyone under the Imperial banner seems impossible."

Ayla nodded. It was a big problem they faced. The Scorpio Alliance was run by men with far too great ambitions, who promised power from without and within for their efforts. If they only could be made to understand how foolish their war against the Imperium was. "I don't have an answer, but then, I'm no diplomat."

"Maybe they'll send you in to woo some of the insurgent leaders," Mihael said. This time, his words had some bite to them. He seems to think of her as willing to do whatever it took for the missions, and while to some extent it was true she wouldn't sacrifice her dignity, it pained her that he seemed to think differently.

"That's not my specialty," Ayla said warmly.

Mihael opened his mouth to protest, but then alerts sounded throughout the ship.

Zahn hopped out of his position on the sofa in the lounge, hustling over to one of the terminals. His face darkened at what he saw. "Alien ships incoming. I need to get to my pilot's chair."

"We all need to get to our stations. Dinner is on pause," Mihael said, setting his bowl on a table.

"After I do all this work," Lycia sighed. "Never fails."

The pirates hurried out of the room and to their stations at the bridge. Ayla followed without anyone saying anything. Even though she might not have had an official place there, she still had the feeling of belonging—more so than being on the *Lyonesse* with the Marines. Lansing had made it difficult on her, but it was neither here nor there.

"Contact the Imperial ship," Mihael said. "Ask them if they're aware of the aliens' presence."

Rams tapped his controls and hailed the *Lyonesse*. He murmured with them through an earpiece, then looked up at Mihael. "They're seeing them as well. But they're closing in, sir, and they're coming in hot with gunports open."

"Ready our weapons," Mihael said. He glanced toward Ayla. "We made some ship upgrades since we last met. Time to see exactly what they can do."

Zahn brought up a glimpse of the alien ships on the viewscreen at the front of the bridge. There were five of them, and if they had the same capabilities as the one ship they'd faced so far, it would be more than a match for the *Peregrine* and *Lyonesse's* combined might.

Ayla was nervous, but she didn't show it. They would have to handle what they could for the ship battle. She'd done her part.

"We only need to be able to escape to hyperspace. There's no reason to make a stand," she said anyway, hoping her words would dampen some of the propensity for aggression the men had.

"The *Lyonesse* captain is saying the same. We'll try to punch a hole, slow them down, and get the heck out of here," Zahn said.

The pilot maneuvered the *Peregrine* forward, weaving through space debris to try to avoid the coming onslaught of alien vessels. With so many Darmarin ships, though, the aliens closed in on them with ease.

Laser blasts fired across the *Peregrine's* starboard bow. More came from the port side.

They had survived their last encounter with the Darmarin, but that had been against only one ship. Now, they faced an entire fleet. But Mihael said they had made some upgrades to the ship. Did that include defensive ones as well? She hoped so.

Some of the Darmarin's shots slammed against the ship, rocking them inside causing the lights to flicker.

"Status," Mihael barked from his captain's chair.

Rams narrowed his eyes, looking at his screen. "All systems are still functioning. They grazed the outside of our hull plating. Nothing to worry about."

"Unless we take a few more hits like that," Ayla said under her breath. The pirates could be far too cavalier for her tastes. Perhaps she should have stayed aboard the Imperial Navy ship.

From where she stood, she could monitor the moving objects on Rams' tactical display. The *Lyonesse* seemed to be right behind them,

Captain Cullen all too content to let the pirates do the heavy lifting of punching a hole through the Darmarin blockade. Why risk your own people when you could let the pirates take the fire?

It didn't stop the *Lyonesse* from firing their weapons at the Darmarin. Smartly, they focused on one ship, the middle left. With its destruction, they could punch a hole through the line of aliens with room to spare as long as they made it through.

Rams seemed to catch wind of the naval ship's strategy, focusing his fire on the same vessel. With the two ships focusing fire, the blasts penetrated the Darmarin's hull, causing an intense explosion that sent the ship sideways and darkening the lights inside as its power died.

Zahn punched the speed higher, pushing through. The Darmarin's blasts continued to pelt them.

"How long until we can attain hyperspace?" Mihael asked.

"Two minutes," Zahn said.

Rams shook his head. "At this rate, we'll be dead in the space in one."

"I thought you said we had nothing to worry about?" Mihael asked.

"That was then. This is now."

Mihael looked like he were about to tear out Rams' throat, but what good would it do? He focused ahead.

"Change course by a few degrees. Do a barrel roll. Throw them off," Ayla said.

Zahn followed her lead, doing as she said, zigging and zagging around the laser fire. It bought them a little time, but maneuvering around would also add time to their departure. Would it be enough?

Ayla couldn't help but hold her breath, clenching her fingers along the railing on the bridge. The ship rocked as it took more fire, jolting Ayla, but she managed to keep her footing.

Suddenly, the *Peregrine* shot into hyperspace, streaks of light growing around them as they left the area of the planetoid behind.

She breathed in, allowing herself to relax. That had been closer than she wanted, but they made it out alive. But what about the *Lyonesse?*

"Did the other ship make it?" Ayla asked.

Rams shook his head. "I can't tell. There was too much interference in the area. Nothing is coming across in our immediate hyperspace lane."

Ayla's heart sank in her chest. Cullen had become her friend. So had Dolame. They were in that ship, and the Darmarin could have done as much or more damage to the *Lyonesse* as they did to the *Peregrine.*

And with the former ship lagging, once the *Peregrine* jumped, the naval vessel could have taken the full brunt of the rest of the Darmarin's force and been destroyed.

Along with most of their data. Ayla moved to the pirate vessel, but the instruments, Dolame's research, and the uploads had all gone aboard the *Lyonesse.* Beyond the people involved, if the Imperial ship didn't make it out, all they would have from this recon mission would be Ayla's observations.

While she was sure she could help some, it wouldn't be nearly enough to justify all their lives.

The bridge went quiet as the news sank in, the pirates seeming to realize that their companions in their fight against the Darmarin may have perished. It was part of the risks of what they did, and Lansing had warned that the Darmarin were prepared for their visit to their planetoid.

Regret sank in for Ayla. She wished she could have cultivated a better relationship with Lansing, but there hadn't been time to overcome his rigid defenses. At least he had begun to respect her by the end of his life.

And Captain Cullen. The captain wanted companionship with her; anything physical hadn't been on the table. She wasn't that kind of girl. But perhaps she could have been sweeter to him in his last moments.

As she thought about the possibility of relationships, Mihael snuck a glance at her from the corner of his eye. He may have thought he was being subtle, but Ayla had too much experience with men to know when they looked at her.

"Did you know them well?" Mihael asked, finally fully turning his attention to her.

"As well as I could on a short mission. I spent more time with you and your crew, so I felt more at home here," Ayla said.

Her words softened Mihael's eyes as he seemed to appreciate her words for the compliment she meant them to be. "You always have a home here, you know."

Rams snorted at the comment.

Mihael turned to his crewman. "What?"

"Your sappiness is unbecoming of being a pirate," Rams said.

"We've been talking about going clean since the last time we met with our friend here. I think it might be time for us to leave our Robeni past behind us," Mihael said.

"I don't much care where the money comes in, so long as it keeps coming," Rams said.

"I like the idea of not having a bounty on my head, personally," Zahn said.

Ayla couldn't help but shake her head. "You boys don't upend your lives for my sake. I'm going to be very busy over the next several months with this war going on. Who knows if I'll be able to cross the spaceways with you again."

A tinge of sadness crept into her belly, giving her a twisting sensation. Was it the deaths of the others she lamented most or her life of always being on the run?

Rams tapped the controls to his station. "Hold on."

"What is it?" Mihael asked.

"A transmission is coming in. It's from the *Lyonesse*. They made it out alive," Rams said.

Ayla's heart skipped a beat. The mission hadn't been in vain. Her people survived. "Tell them we'll see them back at Terra Prime. Oh, and send a message to Lieutenant Lansing: God bless."

EPILOGUE

Ayla waited on one of the top floors of the Terra Prime Intelligence Bureau Headquarters, staring out the window at the cars flying by in the skylanes, as traffic never stopped in the Imperial City.

The conference room had a dozen chairs, with a large holodisplay in the middle for presentations. Jorus, her handler, was with her, as were Lieutenant Lansing and Captain Cullen. They awaited Admiral Daker of the Imperial Navy to join them in a briefing.

The head of the Intelligence Bureau and liaison to the emperor, Pepe Diazo, a slender man with a black stubbled beard and caramel skin, waited with them.

Jorus handed Ayla a fresh cup of coffee in her favorite mug with a picture of a frog on it. Someone had gotten it for her once as a Christmas gift, and though it was an odd choice of a photograph for a coffee mug, it brought her comfort to sip from it.

The dark liquid steamed, the scent of the liquid filling her nostrils —the perks of being back home.

Finally, Daker entered, medals swinging on the breast of his uniform. The military men stood at attention and saluted him, while Ayla, Jorus, and Pepe also stood in respect.

"At ease," Daker said, and the military men relaxed back into their chairs.

The admiral took his chair, sat down, and placed a datapad on the desk. Then, he scrolled through the briefing summary before looking up at everyone again.

Ayla resumed her seat next to Jorus. Her handler gave her a wink, and she couldn't help but roll her eyes playfully back at him.

"Let's see," Admiral Daker said. "We have quite the results from our expedition to the planetoid. Where is our alien expert, though?" He glanced around the table.

On cue, the doors opened, and Dr. Dolame rushed her way inside. She held several different datapads along with folders containing real paper. She worked in strange ways, printing out some of the data onto actual paper, something very few people did.

She said it helped her better not to look at a screen when Ayla had questioned her on it in the lab.

"I'm sorry I'm late," Dr. Dolame said. "I was caught up in some new discoveries which aren't going to make the briefing tablets. It's something you'll all want to know about."

"That's one way to make an entrance," Jorus said under his breath.

Dolame came to the end of the table, nodding toward those present.

"I've seen the technical schematics of the Darmarin vessels and their planetoid base. It will be beneficial for our tactical teams when we come up against their ships in a fight. For that, the Imperium owes the entire crew of the *Lyonesse* a debt of gratitude," Daker said.

"Don't forget our pirate friends," Ayla said.

"Of course, them as well," the Admiral replied, though in a begrudging tone.

"What I have is more important than that," Dolame said.

Mutters in the room quieted as everyone focused their eyes on her.

Dolame took a deep breath, the attention startling her even though she had to have known it was coming. The scientist had a fairly solitary life in her lab and wasn't used to these briefing sessions as the rest of them would have been.

"Upon studying the computer files from the planetoid, we found several incoming transmissions with a different language structure and cadence. These appeared to be orders more than conversations back and forth. These orders included dispatching technology to the Scorpio Alliance and aiding them in building a fleet on one of the outer spiral arm worlds where we previously thought there was no activity," Dolame said.

"Send us the information on that world, and we'll make sure to dispatch a squadron of battlecruisers to the location to make sure those new ships never venture into space," Admiral Daker said in a commanding tone.

Ayla could see why the man had been promoted. With his conviction, she had no doubt he would do as he said swiftly and efficiently.

Pride swelled in her as to being a citizen of the Imperium. The best people rose through the ranks and created the peace and prosperity humanity deserved. She could only be happy to do her part, even if Jorus overworked her from time to time.

Dolame shook her head. "I'm afraid you're missing the important part of what I just said. No offense, Admiral."

"None taken."

"Another language implies there's either another subsect of the Darmarin we're not aware of or, with the corroborating evidence I've uncovered so far, a completely different species entirely," Dolame continued.

Ayla raised a brow. "There are more than one species of alien?"

"More than that, I believe the Darmarin are bred and controlled by this other group. We don't have more information on them, but they keep referring to the Darmarin as harbingers. They are sent ahead to protect this other species, ensure they don't get discovered as our primary attackers, and sow discord here that we might fight amongst ourselves before getting swept up by this greater race. They are the ones seeking our resources. The Darmarin are just doing their bidding."

Mutters escalated across the table.

"What if we show a sign of force?" Lansing asked. "Strike at the heart of these aliens and show them humanity is a force to be reckoned with."

Dolame pursed her lips. "It all sounds well and good, but we don't even know where this other species comes from, what they're like, or anything. We only have basic constructs of language, and what appears to be some designs or technology are not in line with what our AI system comes to expect from Darmarin origin."

"We're facing an even bigger coalition than we thought," Ayla said. Goosebumps appeared on her body, and a chill ran through her. There was too much out there they didn't know, and it looked like the Imperium was in for the most difficult fight they could imagine.

"Dr. Dolame," Admiral Daker said. "Please, forward this information to my office so my analysts can review it. Anything else you can glean would be helpful."

"Of course."

With that, the admiral stood. "We have a lot to think about and trying times in the months ahead. A job well done to all of you. The Imperium gives her thanks. Get some rest while you can. We'll need your service sooner rather than later."

Daker shook hands with some of the men, gave Ayla a cordial nod, and made his way out. The others filed with them, and Dolame waved to Ayla on the way out the door. After a time, only Jorus and her remained the lone representatives of the agency whose headquarters they met in.

Jorus sat patiently, tapping on his datapad before looking up at Ayla.

"You're waiting to tell me something," Ayla said.

"Astute as ever." Jorus chuckled.

"It's going to be something I don't like." Ayla narrowed her eyes.

"Got it in one," Jorus said. He adjusted his coat before sliding the datapad across to her. "I know we've been pushing you hard lately, but are you ready for your next mission?"

* * *

AYLA RIN WILL RETURN.

THE CONVERSION OF AYLA RIN

A DRONE HOVERED OVER AYLA RIN'S APARTMENT BALCONY, CATCHING her eye through the thin white curtains, partially blocking the sunlight from where she sat on her couch. Ayla jumped to her feet, having faced too many attacks from flying drones in recent days to want to risk being shot at with a laser bolt, even in the safety of her home on Terra Prime.

While security in Victory City had been tightened in recent days after the revelation of Emperor Grigor having been kidnapped and replaced by a clone even under the faithful watch of the Emperor's Guard, her instincts she'd been programmed with during her agency training wouldn't allow her to be lax when presented with any potential threat.

Very few in the Imperium had her personal address. The apartment was listed under a fictitious name. Whenever she had to make an order for her personal shopping or rooftop garden, it was tracked, and she would have been aware of any delivery.

The drone hovered for a moment, casting a slight shadow, and appeared to deposit something. She wasn't expecting any packages. Was it a bomb? Should she alert the rest of the building's residents?

She reached for a small holdout pistol she had under her couch cushion, gripping the handle and pulling it up as she kept herself out of the direct line of sight from the window.

Perhaps she was paranoid, but these days, with the Scorpio Alliance being such a threat, one had to be to survive.

The drone dropped the package, leaving it on her balcony. Ayla wondered if she should call in a bomb squad, but if this were a simple misunderstanding, she didn't want to force all of the residents to evacuate the building.

She crept toward the balcony door, keeping her eyes glued to the glass to see if there was any movement. The drone flew away as soon as it had come and didn't appear to be hovering anywhere nearby where it could cast a shadow or be coming back for another pass.

Once she approached the door, she brought herself out into the open, laser pistol in hand, ready for action if need be.

The cityscape in front of her looked as busy as ever, with skycars zooming back and forth, people walking in the tubes and on the streets down below, and other large buildings filled with apartments and offices standing across from her home. There was no sign of the drone. Nothing seemed out of the ordinary.

The package on the ground was small, appearing to be a paper envelope with some padding. With modern technology, anything could conceal a small explosive, but the package didn't look much like a bomb.

Ayla opened the door and picked up the package. It was light in weight and had some bumps. Whoever had sent it didn't leave their return address on the outside, lending to her suspicion, but it seemed there was no immediate danger. She placed her pistol on her balcony table, where she liked to sit and get some sunlight when relaxing at home.

She flopped into the chair, still looking at the package, wondering if she should open it.

Curiosity got the best of her, and Ayla ripped open the package by a tab toward the top of it. She did so slowly, careful in case she might find something strange inside. Nothing seemed out of the ordinary, so she turned the opening to the table, letting the contents fall out.

Inside was a small piece of paper with bad handwriting on it, as well as what appeared to be a necklace with several dark wooden beads and a carved cross at the end. She understood the cross symbology as part of the Christian faith, but why would someone send her a necklace like this? What was its purpose?

She picked up the piece of paper, reading the inscription.

Ayla, I appreciated working with you on our last mission and our discussions on God, demons, and the Xenos. This is a rosary. You can look up how to use it on the nets. It can be used to fight demons, both internal and external.

Sincerely,

Lt. Rod Lansing.

Ayla stifled a breath, taken aback at the gift. Though she had seen the change when Lansing had gone from what appeared to be a disdain for her to a grudging respect, she hadn't thought that he remotely liked her, let alone *appreciated* working with her.

Though she had never been religious, the gift was thoughtful, given their brief discussions on the divine and how it related to the universe at large. Lansing was a deeply spiritual man, in addition to his unwavering loyalty to the Imperium, something she respected about him. They were alike in many ways, willing to do anything to defend humanity and their way of life. She could be as rigid as he was in her ways.

Had she been too rigid? She clutched the rosary in her hands, letting the beads fall between her fingers. There was something comforting about having it. Part of her had always wondered if there was a God up in the universe watching over her, protecting her. It sure seemed like the Imperium had been blessed somehow. In different times, there had even been a movement to deify the Imperial line, to call the Emperor a God-Emperor, but Emperor Treinen IV quickly ended any talk of that. He had been a humble man for all of his power.

It was something she would consider. Lansing, while firm in his belief, didn't press her too hard about it and didn't seem to judge her thoughts on God one way or another. He'd spoken little but said a lot with the way he lived and with the gift he gave her.

Regardless, Ayla felt the need to thank him. If she could, the best way would be in person. Picking up her pistol, she headed back inside her apartment to see what she could do about discovering where Lansing might be if the man hadn't been redeployed from Terra Prime already.

* * *

TRACKING LANSING HAD BEEN EASY. He had a military apartment not far from the parade grounds outside the city. Like herself as a special agent, the elite squad of The Emerald Array all had chips embedded in them for tracking—for their safety in case of capture and in case something happened where they went rogue and needed to be hunted down. She hoped it wouldn't happen, though some in the agency still thought of her as rogue after her recent escapades. It would take time to repair those relationships.

The tracking revealed Lansing was a man of habit when he wasn't deployed on assignment. He visited the cathedral often, pious as he was, but he also visited a local coffee house daily when he wasn't on duty. This place was known to be expensive, using beans from the southern continent grown on slopes of a mountain range that had a natural fertilizer from a goat population. She'd read a brochure about it once, and her eidetic memory did the rest.

He always came by the coffee house at about the same hour, which made it easy for Ayla to park herself at a table, get a latte, and read a novel on her datapad until he arrived. It was like any other stakeout, but due to her genetically enhanced senses, she was keenly aware of her surroundings.

Lansing opened the door like clockwork, and she could tell from the measured footballs of his marine standard-issue boots that it was him. She didn't have to look up, but she did, hoping to catch his eye.

The gruff soldier with a cybernetic eyepiece noticed her immediately. The red hair made it difficult for her to hide at times, though oddly enough, as a spy, she found that her natural beauty and distinctive features often made her less scrutinized than some of the more plain-looking agents. It was odd how human psychology worked sometimes.

"Ms. Rin," Lansing said, veering from the line of people gathered to order their drinks to stand by her table. "I wasn't expecting to see you here."

"It's a big city, and the two of us happened to run into each other," Ayla said with a smile.

"You sought me out intentionally." His gruff voice always came across as severe and scrutinizing.

Ayla set her datapad down. "You got me. I came here to see you, actually."

"How did you—" Lansing stopped himself mid-sentence and shook his head. "Nevermind. You have Imperial resources. "What can I do for you?'

"Get your coffee and come sit down a moment. I'll wait." Ayla shooed him in the direction of the line.

Lansing complied, a good soldier following orders, even if she wasn't in his chain of command. He made his way to the front of the line as the barista took each order and eventually returned with a steaming mug of coffee.

"Black coffee?" Ayla asked.

"Strong. Pure caffeine. I don't need anything else." Lansing helped himself to a seat across from her.

She liked to cut the coffee flavor with something creamier. But to each their own. Ayla took a sip of her latte, which this establishment served in cups that seemed wider, more like bowls than most. It required her to pick it up with both hands and set it back down before doing anything else.

"What did you want to see me about?" Lansing asked. He blew the steam away from his cup to cool it.

"Your gift," Ayla said.

Lansing raised a brow. "I hope it didn't offend you."

"Not at all. It was thoughtful. I wanted to thank you. I looked up the rosary on the nets, and it seems to be a pretty detailed prayer and reflection. There are even different meditations for different days of the week based on certain details of Christ's life?" Ayla asked, having read the matter but wanting some confirmation to see if she was on the right track.

"Indeed. Today, for instance, would be the Luminous Mysteries."

"I see. I'm not sure I'll use it, but it gives me something to consider. Given all we've seen, how vast this universe is, how much evil truly does exist… I definitely can conclude a God of some sort exists who created definite rules for what is good and true."

Lansing grunted and took a first sip of his coffee. His human eye seemed to relax when he tasted it. Funny how people reacted to the beverage.

"Well, thank you, regardless. I'll keep it in my apartment and hang it where I can see it. At the very least, it'll be a memory of serving together," Ayla said. She offered a small smile.

Lansing didn't smile in return. He hardly showed any emotion. "I do my prayers at the cathedral before coming here. I'm guessing you already know this."

Ayla shrugged.

"I'm hearing rumblings there will be a new assignment for The Emerald Array soon. With the war spreading to so many sectors, I'm not sure where we'll be deployed." Lansing said. He didn't sound like he enjoyed the time in limbo. He was a man who liked certainty.

"For me, I'm hoping I get at least a couple of weeks off. It's been a hellish schedule. Though we do what we have to for the Imperium." Ayla touched her cup but didn't pick it up.

"I will add your desire for rest to my prayer petitions," Lansing said.

He was singular-minded; she'd give him that. "Thank you." With this, Ayla took another long sip of her drink. With so much effort to pick it up by two hands, she wanted to make it worth the while.

Lansing made no move to leave. He drank his coffee with her. The conversation was sparse but not awkward. It was good to spend some downtime together. Ayla found the more she got to know him, the more she enjoyed him for who he was. While he could be terse and gruff, he had honor, loyalty, and strength—a perfect marine.

Once the coffee was finished, they both moved to stand together.

"I'm off duty," Lansing said. "I wouldn't mind taking a walk and escorting you to your apartment if it's nearby."

Was he flirting with her? Ayla couldn't tell if it was that or if it was an innate desire to be protective. Either way, she found it sweet. "You're on. Follow me."

She moved to the door and pushed it open for them to head outside.

* * *

Before exiting, Lansing moved ahead and held the door for Ayla. It was a small, classic gesture, but Ayla found herself impressed by it.

"Thank you," Ayla said, stepping through to the street outside.

The city was just as bustling as before, and traffic got worse in the mid-day rush of people heading to their various places of work or leisure. Ayla was content to be close enough to her residence to avoid having to get into a car—ground or sky.

Lansing was out the door a moment after her, glancing both ways down the street. "Which direction is your home?"

"This way." Ayla pointed to the northbound direction of the sidewalk.

The two started walking together when a large *crack* echoed through the city streets. People gasped, a woman screamed.

Ayla's chest flared with pain like it was hit by one of the ground cars in oncoming traffic. The *cracking* noise had hit her. She fell over against the wall beside her, hitting her head. Her vision blurred, and she became disoriented as she slumped to the sidewalk.

Lansing crouched beside her. "Ayla! Ayla! Can you hear me?" He grabbed his comm unit and called. "Medical emergency. We are on Sivion Street in front of the South Terra Coffee House." He glanced upward toward the top of buildings. "There's an active shooter. He's on the roof of the Credit One Bank building. I'm too far away to assist."

Ayla's life flashed before her eyes as the world blurred around her. Lansing's voice sounded very distant. The pain intensified. What happened to her? It sounded like there was an assassin somewhere.

"Stay with me, Ayla. Focus." Lansing's voice called out, but she could hardly see him anymore.

Her vision went dark, but at the last moment, she thought she saw a figure with light surrounding him. Was it a trick of her eye, her mind not able to see Lansing? Or something else?

She lost consciousness before finding the answer.

* * *

AYLA AWOKE in a hospital bed some hours later. She'd been hooked up to monitoring machines, though the medical staff appeared to be elsewhere. Lansing sat in a chair beside her, clutching a rosary, head bowed. When she stirred, he looked up at her.

"You're awake," Lansing said.

"I am. But I feel like I've been parked on by a flitter. What happened?" Ayla tried to sit herself up, but it hurt, so she resigned herself to her uncomfortable position in bed.

Lansing let out a long breath. "You should rest and recover, but there was an assassination attempt on you. Don't worry, the shooter was caught. It was a Scorpio Alliance sympathizer who apparently tracked you here from the Zenda colony world."

"He missed," Ayla said wryly.

"He didn't." Lansing cracked what passed for a smile by his standards. He held up the rosary in his hands. The cross and a few of the beads had been blasted off. "You had this in a pouch connected to a strap on your purse. It was in the perfect place over your chest where the bullet would have gone through. If it hadn't been there, you'd be dead now. It was a miracle."

Goosebumps appeared on Ayla's arms, and she couldn't help but shiver. The rosary had saved her. She'd already been thinking about the existence of God before this incident, but she had to admit this was more than a coincidence.

"Funny."

"Hmm?"

"Before I blacked out, I saw a figure with a bright light around him. I thought it was just you reflecting in the sunlight with my blurred vision, but it might have been something else," Ayla said.

Lansing nearly leaped from his chair, his one human eye gone wide as he took her by her hand, pressing the broken rosary between his and her skin. "You encountered Christ. Or an angel. Perhaps St. Michael. This needs to be reported to the clergy at the cathedral. I can attest that this was a miraculous moment."

Ayla's head started spinning again. This was too much for her. She was exhausted from the trauma her body endured, miracle or not. "Hold your horses, Lieutenant. I've never seen you so excited except when you're in battle. But I'm not going anywhere for a little while. Why don't you tell me a little more about your faith? I'm here to listen and have some time. I want to know what I should believe and who just saved me."

A doctor came by to check on her and seemed pleased she was awake. The visit was brief as he took readings of her vitals while Lansing sat back down. Once the doctor left, Lansing looked at her with serious intent.

"It started with a man named Jesus Christ. He lived on Old Earth thousands of years ago. And if you thought what happened to you was miraculous..."

THE LONE SURVIVOR

By Blaine Pardoe

This story takes place prior to The Hidden Emperor and Into The Black.

THE TRAIL THEY MARCHED ON WAS ACTUALLY A RIDGE. FORMED, HE HAD been told, by a crack in an ancient glacier. Corporal Wixner Richards didn't care how it was formed. The whole patrol seemed like a waste of time. Yes, there were "rebels" operating in the area, but none had dared tangle with a fully armored platoon. *They are really little more than terrorists, cowards who set off bombs and issue defiant statements.* The weekly intel briefings seemed to think they were more of a threat, but Wixner didn't fully trust those. *Show me an intelligent intel officer and I will show you a myth.*

The Imperium had been at peace for decades, or so the media claimed. There were always little uprisings, though, just enough to remind the military high command that they needed to be vigilant. The biggest threats seemed to come from within. *Somebody has to be funding this Travas Militant Front (TMF), getting them weapons and explosives.* No one seemed to have an idea who was behind those efforts. It didn't matter to the locals. The Marines were here. *We bring peace through superior firepower.* It wasn't the official motto of the Marines, but one that was commonly accepted.

The ridgeline was about ten meters wide and covered with trees and rocks. On either side was a steep, forty-five-degree slope covered in rocks and brush. To the right, a swamp, black, deep, and brackish, impassable from what he could tell. To the left, a kilometer-long slope down to a small lake with another ridge line rising in the distance.

"I'm not sure why they have us parading around out here," griped Private Slotchez over the close-net discreet channel in their power armor. "Seems like we'd be more intimidating back in the city."

Richards' eyes darted around the tactical display of his helmet, doing what he had been trained for, looking for possible threats. "Your heard the LT. They say that the TMF operates out of this region. We're here to demonstrate that we can get close to their homes and loved ones. You know, put the fear of God into them." Just talking about the TMF made him want to check his surroundings. His tactical display gave him a good feed of the platoon, marching single file along the ridge, but no signs of any other life forms.

"They aren't going to shoot at us," Slotchez muttered. "I mean seriously, we're Marines. We're sporting the latest tech, Mark XI armor, Craybach Plasma burst 300 laser rifle, Kamer Sabers…only a moron would dare engage us. You've seen the intel dumps. Their tech is old."

"I've seen slug-tossers punch through our armor." They had been shown that during Basic.

"I saw that too. They have to get close for those antiques to hurt. We'll see and kill them long before they get in tight. Besides, word is they aren't organized. Too many chiefs…that's my take on them."

The bravado was understood. It came with being a Marine. The lack of big wars made everyone in the military a bit egotistic. Peace had a way of dulling even the sharpest of blades. Richards understood that all too well. Previous generations of his family had fought and died in the real wars, the old ones, back before the Great Peace. He'd been to their grave sites, said the prayers, and been told the stories of their gallantry every Heritage Day. Wixner's family was one of those who had always served the Imperium in war and peace.

"Can the chatter, Slouch," snapped the voice of Sergeant Dalton, using Slotchez's nickname. "We are here to do the bidding of the Imperium. Your opinion on political matters doesn't mean squat until you make officer, and I don't see that happening in either of our lifetimes."

Richards cracked a smile. It was always better to hear someone else get verbally pummeled by Dalton.

As they moved along the ridge, the pathway between the two slopes narrowed down to five meters. It made Richards a little edgy. *There's less room to deploy if we have to. Slotchez is probably right, but there was always a chance that—*

The explosion some fifteen meters in front of him cut his thinking off like a swing of his Kamer saber. The concussion of the blast threw Slotchez back into him and sent both of them cascading into Harnez who had been holding the rear of their patrol. Richards felt his neck ache from the blast and for a moment, he was stunned, laying on his back with Slotchez halfway on top of him.

Dalton's voice came on the discreet channel. "Noble wing formation, form up on me!" There was no time for thinking, only action. Hours of drilling and practicing made changing their formation a matter of muscle memory. Rolling in his power armor, Richards got to his knees, then rose. As he did, he reached down and pulled up Slotchez. "Come on, we're on the right!" The two of them shifted to the down the steep slope, only to suddenly have laser bolts of crimson rise out of the swamp up at them. One fiery red bolt glanced off of the cerro-fiber armor of his left leg, leaving an ugly black scar where it had struck. He dove behind a boulder as another explosion went off behind him on the far side of the ridge.

Using his eye movement, he adjusted his visor's targeting system, looking for a heat signature, but wasn't getting any. "I don't see them," he muttered, half to himself, half to Slotchez. A trio of bolts shot up out of the muddy swamp, hitting the rock formation he was huddled behind. The superheated plasma blasts cracked and exploded off bits of the rock, raining it down on the two of them as he ducked his head back down. He returned fire at what he presumed was the source. It was impossible to tell if he had hit anyone.

Then he understood. "Sergeant, they are using the mud on the right to hide their IR sigs," he called out.

"We've got fast-moving boats out on that pond hitting on the left," Private Redalno called out. "Damn, those are big guns!" The crack-whine of the larger lasers now joined the cacophony of sounds of the fighting as the Marines tried to find targets and return fire.

Another explosion went off, this time right where they had been on the top of the ridge. Dirt and rocks rained down on them. Richards glanced back and saw Harnez stagger through the gray haze of the smoke. His power armor was blackened by the blast, and there were several cracks in it. Worse, he was missing most of his left arm. The flesh had been severed but hung like a pendulum, swinging at the shoulder joint, held on by the ballistic inner-weave of the armor. Bloody bits of flesh dripped from the dangling limb as he staggered a few steps and collapsed above them, sliding down to a few meters away.

Richards reached out as shots peppered the ground around him, grabbed a service hook on Harnez's armor, and pulled him behind the rock he was using for cover. He pressed his armored finger on the neckpiece of the armor on the sync-plate so he could see the readings. Harnez was alive, but probably not for long. His life signs, displayed in his visor, were dropping fast.

"Harnez is down," he transmitted. "I need Foxx" Foxx was their corpsman. He had the medical gear that might save his comrade's life.

"Foxx is toast. So's the LT, Warton, and Hickers," Sergeant Dalton replied as another explosion rocked the ridge line.

They got the Lieutenant too...this is bad.

"We have to move!" came Earna's panicked voice.

"We've got good cover here," Sergeant Dalton said. "We'll redeploy and form up on the right side of the ridge and use the boulders there for cover. Left wing, fall back by pairs to the right side of the ridge, form up a tight circle. I want eyes on that swamp. Find us some targets to kill."

"How about some air support?" Corporal Raver's voice asked.

"Long range comms are not being picked up," Dalton said in a half-cursing voice. "We're on our own here." There was something in the way that he said those words that sent a chill down Richards' spine. Removing his finger from the press plate, he reached down and applied pressure to the bloody stump of Harnez's arm, more out of desperation than actually knowing what to do. Blood oozed over his armored fingers, signs of a struggle that he could not hope to win. Slotchez rose and fired wildly down the hillside into the swamp, hopefully providing suppression fire.

Dalton's voice returned in his earpiece, this time breathing fast and ragged. "We can hold this ground. Richards, I want you to sprint back, get out of jamming range, and get second platoon up here." A muffled explosion on the left side of the ridge rained down leaves from the tall trees above him.

"Sir, I'd rather stay with the unit and fight," he said firmly. His platoon was his family. The Imperial Marines were brothers and sisters.

"Do as you are ordered, Corporal. You're our fastest runner. If we move, we are a big target. One Marine, alone, running like all hell, they aren't going to waste time with you. Backtrack down the trail. Get out of jamming range and call in some relief. We can hold until you get back."

"Yes, Sergeant," he said, then nudged Slotchez. "You have to apply pressure to his wound," he said. Slotchez bent down and the two swapped hands on Harnez.

"Haul ass," Slotchez said.

Richards dripped his head once in a lonely nod, then started his run, heading diagonally up to the top of the ridge and back the way they had come. Laser bolts raced in the surrounding air. One hit a tree in front of him, causing it to explode, sending big pieces of wood with hundreds of splinters into him, dancing off his armor. Richards' didn't break stride, even for that. *They are all counting on me.* An explosion rocked the ground behind him, the concussion making his entire power armor suit seem to throb, but he didn't falter.

The sounds of the battle drifted off behind him, and for a moment, he thought himself safe. Then, a figure jumped out from behind a tree, right into the middle of the trail. It was a woman wearing a hodge-podge of armor plates more befitting an antique store than being pushed into combat. The laser bolt she had unleashed a scarlet pulse that hit his left chest plate full on as he ran right towards her.

Damage indicators flickered in his visor, but Richards ignored them. Mid-stride, he raised his laser rifle and fired a full spread. Three bolts missed, and three found their mark, hitting the woman in one arm and in her chest. The super-heated plasma hitting human tissue made for a crimson mist explosion as her body flew backward. He sprinted right past her as white wisps of smoke rolled from what had been her upper torso. Richards didn't care. She had tried to kill and had paid the Marine's price for her folly.

He tried to signal every fifty meters, hoping to pick up on the company's command channel but got nothing but a buzzing noise on those frequencies. *Damned TMF – who gave them that kind of jamming gear?* His legs were numb, and his lungs struggled to get in the air. His armor was turning into a furnace as he ran, but he could not stop.

He was a full seven kilometers from the battle site when he finally got a signal through. "First platoon has been attacked and is fully defensive," he said, gasping for breath. "We need immediate relief."

"Identify yourself," came back a stern female voice.

"Corporal Richards, RM7091," he said, finally stopping. "Ping my position. I am seven klicks from my platoon."

"Where is Lieutenant Billingham?"

"Dead," he said, still breathing hard. "I need reinforcements. We have to get back there before they are slaughtered."

For a few moments, there was no response. Richards wondered if his last message had gotten through. He was about to query them to see if they had heard him a male voice came on. "We're coming to you right now, Corporal."

"Sir, I need to get back to them," he said.

"We're coming with two platoons and will be there shortly. We need you to guide us in."

No! I need to be with them. "Sir, I—"

"Hold tight, Marine. Help is on the way."

* * *

THE WAIT WAS ARDUOUS. Three times, he considered breaking his orders, starting back a few apprehensive meters at a time, only to stop. *Remember your orders. Damn them!* Rumbles of explosions in the distance seemed to die off, which was also sickening. He tried to communicate with his platoon but had no luck. The jamming was still in place.

Finally, the second platoon arrived, moving fast. Their gray-green armor looked like a snake as they came up the ridge single file. Just past the point was Captain Blucher, his name and rank stenciled over his left breastplate. "Richards," he acknowledged, not even pausing as Wixner fell in next to him, jogging at long last back to where his platoon was. "What are we up against?"

"The trail narrows up ahead. We were getting hit on both flanks. On the right, they were using the bog to mask their IR signatures. On the left, they had speedboats with some heavy laser power. They had zeroed us in with artillery. The Leuitenant is dead. Sergeant Dalton has command. He had the platoon shift to the right flank. It had better cover." Once more, the temperature in his power armor started rising, and his interweave was soaked with his hot sweat. Richards didn't care. He needed to get back. As he got his breath, he wondered and worried how the fight had gone.

"Alright then," Captain Blucher said. "When we are a kilometer out, we go down the right side of the ridge. I want us in two columns, give us twenty meters' distance in case they bring the steel rain. Let's get in there and save our brothers and sisters." They were the right words but did little to assuage the feeling of dread that was growing in the dark recesses of Richards' mind.

As they got close, the second platoon split up. Smoke snaked skyward from several areas, almost like funeral pyres. Richards sprinted ahead, giving visual direction with his hands. A few minutes later, he saw the site of the battle.

There were a few trees left standing. Those that did were likely to die from their scars. Charred stumps jutted skyward, belching smoke almost obscuring the big red sun starting to set. The ground, covered with scrub brushes, was cratered, the flora tossed about in dying clumps. He spied the rock where he and Slotchez had dug in. The large boulders were fractured and super-heated by countless plasma bolt hits. He saw the limp form of Harnez; his helmet melted in squarely...a close-range kill shot.

A few meters away, under a limb, he spotted an armored leg. Moving over to it, he strained to pull the heavy bough off of the body. It was Slotchez. At first, he thought he was dead too, but as he rolled him over, his brother Marine moaned. In his hand was his Kamer Saber; its ultra-fine filament edge had been battered to the point of inoperability. There were no dead around the wounded Marine, meaning that their attackers had taken the dead and wounded with them. There were drag marks in the churned-up soil, and dull maroon splotches that he assumed were blood. *I should have been here.*

"Where'd they get you?" he asked, reaching in at the neck and hitting Slotchez's emergency egress control. The claps that held the power armor into place hissed and then snapped free.

"Where didn't they get me?" he muttered, then coughed.

The second platoon was moving fast to secure the hillside. So far, it looked as if the TMF had departed. Richards pulled off his injured comrade's battered armor and helmet. He had a shot that had melted through the seven layers of armored protection on his side, burning and searing his lower abdomen. The wound was flanked by cracked black skin and charred and oozing body fluid, but it didn't seem to bleed externally.

"How bad?" Slotchez asked, his face wincing in agony.

"You're not dead yet," Richards told him. He switched to an open channel. "Corpsman! Ping on me!"

Captain Blucher's voice came back. "We don't have our corpsman, he's in the infirmary with Fireplague."

"I've got a wounded man here. He's still alive and needs help!"

"We'll need to signal for an extract. Dooley, get that signal booster up so we can call in the dropsled! Make it happen yesterday!"

This time, when Slotchez coughed, it came with blood. *He's got more than this wound happening.* "You're going to be okay," he tried to assure him.

"They came out of the swamp, around a hundred of them. We got a lot of them, but they tore us a new asshole. Dalton went down. Pinko took command, tried to get us huddled into one spot. I lost Harnez right after you left."

"Don't talk," he said.

"Dropsled is inbound," Captain Blucher signal, his voice booming in his helmet.

"It was hand-to-hand at the end. Someone dropped that damn tree on me." He seemed to be looking around. "I heard Pinko say they were overrun."

"We're going to get you out of here."

"You pick me up, and I will fall apart," Slotchez replied. "We could have used you here, brother."

Guilt – crushing, all-consuming, washed over him. It was like a Tanzer Constrictor Eel, making it hard for him to breathe. "They wouldn't let me come back. The Sergeant made me go."

"I know. Still—could have used you." He whetted his lips and winced again. "I'm starting to feel cold. If I don't make it, you need to tell my parents...what I did."

Shock. He remembered studying it and remembered it was bad. "Hold on, buddy. I'm right here with you."

"Wish you'd brought a medkit," he said as his voice trailed off. Slotchez's eyelids fluttered, then closed.

"No! Hang with me! He shook his comrade's body, barely moving it with the armor still on the limbs. There was no response. Richards felt his jaw clench. Tears tried to escape the corners of his eyes, but he refused to let them.

I won't let this happen again. I can't. I'm going to learn to be a Corpsman. If I had been, he and Harnez might still be alive. I swear, I will not go through this ever again. Saving lives is far more important than taking them.

ALSO BY JON DEL ARROZ

The Adventures Of Baron Von Monocle:

For Steam And Country

The Blood Of Giants

The Fight For Rislandia

The Iron Wedding

The Steam Knight

The Crystal Conspiracy

The Nano Templar Series

Justified

Sanctified

Glorified

The Aryshan War

The Stars Entwined

The Stars Asunder

The Stars Rejoined

Colony Launch

The Roles We Play

The Terran Imperium Chronicles

The Immortal Edge

Milton Keynes UK
Ingram Content Group UK Ltd.
UKHW031135291024
2429UKWH00006B/299

9 781951 837617